Demetrius crossed his muscular arms. "Perhaps hiring you was a mistake—"

"No—" Zoe bit back her next words, but it was too late. Demetrius's brows had lifted at her sudden outburst. "I mean, we have an agreement in writing."

"And you didn't think that I would leave myself a loophole—a way out if the need arose?"

Who was this man? And what had happened to the laid-back Demetrius?

Her gut told her to get out now. That she was getting in far too deep with a man who still had a hold on her heart.

To complicate matters further, she had no job to return to. She'd already resigned from her position as interior designer for the island's most prominent furniture store. And most importantly this job paid well—well enough to pay her mother's bills.

Zoe was stuck.

"You still haven't answered my question. Why did you hire me?" She watched him carefully, not sure what sort of reaction to expect.

"I wanted the best for this job. And you are the best on the island."

Was he serious? He thought she was the best? A warmth swirled in her chest and rose to warm her cheeks. Their gazes connected and held. Her heart thudded harder, faster. She refused to acknowledge that his words meant anything to her. She was over him. Past him.

"So you just expect us to work together like…like nothing ever happened?"

Dear Reader,

Thanks to an overwhelming volume of reader requests, I'm thrilled to share with you the second book in the Twin Princes of Mirraccino duet. This book tells the story of the Crown Prince…and the princess of his heart.

They both have an important lesson to learn—that the heart has a will of its own and doesn't care if it's a convenient time, politically correct, or if others disapprove. It loves who it loves. The problem is, the mind worries about all of those pesky details. And at times it can be quite a struggle.

Such is the case for Demetrius and Zoe. Their problems were stacked against them from the start, and ultimately they failed their first attempt at happily-ever-after. Now, with Christmas in the air, they both think they are over each other, they've moved on. But there's one tiny hitch…

They're still married!

Can the magic of the season heal their scarred hearts? Or is the distance between them too far to bridge over a Christmas cookie or two?

I hope you enjoy returning to Mirraccino as much as I did. And if you didn't get a chance to read the first book in this holiday duet you can find *A Princess by Christmas* online at numerous outlets.

Happy reading!

Jennifer

THE PRINCE'S CHRISTMAS VOW

BY
JENNIFER FAYE

First published in Great Britain 2015
by Mills & Boon, an imprint of Harlequin (UK) Limited,
Eton House, 18-24 Paradise Road, Richmond, Surrey, TW9 1SR

© 2015 Jennifer F. Stroka

ISBN: 978-0-263-25919-3

Printed and bound in Great Britain
by CPI Antony Rowe, Chippenham, Wiltshire

Award-winning author **Jennifer Faye** pens fun, heart-warming romances. Jennifer has won the RT Reviewers' Choice Best Book Award, is a Top Pick author and has been nominated for numerous awards. Now living her dream, she resides with her patient husband, one amazing daughter—the other remarkable daughter is off chasing her own dreams—and two spoiled cats. She'd love to hear from you via her website: jenniferfaye.com.

Visit the Author Profile page at millsandboon.co.uk for more titles.

To my readers…
I am so blessed to have the most amazing readers,
some who have become dear friends.
I greatly appreciate your friendly notes, unfailing
support and daily company on social media.
Thank you.

You all are amazing!

Read both books in this royal duet:
The Prince's Christmas Vow
November 2015
and
A Princess by Christmas
October 2014

CHAPTER ONE

THE PLAN WAS in motion.

Though suddenly, it didn't sound like such a good idea.

Demetrius Castanavo, the Crown Prince of the Mirraccino Islands, shrugged off the worrisome feeling as he stepped out of the air-conditioned black limousine. Nothing was going to go wrong. He glanced at the clear blue sky, appreciating this last bit of good weather before it cooled down in the weeks leading up to Christmas.

Demetrius buttoned his charcoal-gray suit jacket, gave each sleeve a tug and then straightened his shoulders. Today he must look his best. It was imperative.

A bright camera flash momentarily blinded him.

He blinked, regaining his focus. The media coverage had begun. He restrained a sigh. Instead he lifted his chin and forced his lips into a well-practiced smile.

Demetrius, the royal playboy, was no more. His days of nonchalance and bucking the system were over. Now he was intent on becoming a proper and worthy heir to the Mirraccino throne. It was, after all, his birthright—whether he desired it or not.

And now he was about to participate in a very important interview that would help shape his new, improved public image—one he hoped would sway the residents of the Mirraccino nation to support his inevitable rise to the throne.

His gaze settled on an impressive set of steps that led to a historic mansion. At the top was an expansive landing with large, white columns amid the backdrop of blue shuttered windows. The place was a timeless beauty. He was glad they were going to save this building by revitalizing it.

There was just one snag in his well-thought-out plan—Zoe.

His estranged wife.

But that situation would be resolved soon—very soon.

The head of his security detail leaned in close and whispered, "The reporter is waiting for you on the landing, Your Royal Highness."

Demetrius shoved the disturbing thoughts of his estranged wife to the back of his mind. He'd deal with her tomorrow. "Good. As soon as I meet with him, we have to get moving if we're going to stay on schedule today."

"Sir, the reporter, it's a woman."

"*Sì.* I remember now." Demetrius needed to keep his head in this game instead of wondering how Zoe would react when she saw him again.

Demetrius swiftly climbed the steps that fanned out, covering a large area while adding to the building's charm. He'd definitely made the right decision by insisting the all-access ramp be constructed on the side of the building, readily accessible yet not losing the building's aesthetic appeal.

His vision was to marry the building's beauty with functionality. They were doing well with the functionality. The beauty would be Zoe's area of expertise. And tomorrow would be her first day on the job.

Off to the far side of the landing stood a short, slender brunette. Her makeup was a bit heavy for his tastes, but he reasoned that it must have something to do with spending so much time in front of the television cameras. Interviews were one of his least favorite tasks, but at times they were a necessity—like now.

When his advisors had unanimously agreed this was the best way for him to overhaul his scandalous youthful past, they had also assured him that agreeing to the one-on-one interview would be the best way to give the citizens access to him—to let them know that he was serious about being a caring, involved ruler. Though he'd rather keep his distance from the paparazzi, Demetrius had to admit that in this one particular instance, they may in fact come in handy—quite handy indeed.

He reached the landing and turned to the reporter. Greetings were quick and formal. Demetrius had every intention of keeping things moving along at a brisk pace. He knew the more time he spent with the media, the more they'd learn. And in his experience, that was never a good thing. He wanted to control the flow of information, not the other way around.

Ms. Carla Russo, the face of Mirraccino's entertainment news, held a microphone. "Before we begin, I wondered if you might have an announcement for our viewers."

"I do have news—"

"Oh, good. We've been hearing all sorts of rumors, and the viewers would really like confirmation that you've decided upon a princess."

What?

The cameraman moved closer. Demetrius's throat constricted. They knew about Zoe? No. Impossible. The reporter was on a hunting expedition. Pure and simple. Anything for a sensational headline. Well, he wasn't about to give her anything to chase. Nothing at all.

With practiced skill, Demetrius forced his lips into a smile. "I can assure you there is no princess in my near future."

"That's not what we've heard. There are rumors floating about that someone special has caught your attention. Could you share her name with us?"

Maybe the reporter did know something about Zoe, after all. Though the palace employees had all signed confidentiality agreements, there could still be a leak. A delivery person? A guest? There was always room for someone who'd slipped through the cracks. But obviously, whatever this woman knew wasn't much or she'd be throwing out names and facts.

He couldn't lose control of this interview. It wasn't just the building that was about to get a fresh lease on life. If his plan succeeded, their futures would both have makeovers. After all, he'd been putting off getting on with his royal duties long enough now. He'd grown. He'd learned. And now he was becoming the man he should have been all along.

With his twin brother, Alexandro, now married and spending a lot of time abroad in his wife's homeland, more responsibilities had befallen the king. But the king was not in the best of health. The physicians kept warning him to slow down. And that's why Demetrius's plan just had to work. He didn't want his father to have a heart attack or worse.

The first part of his plan included gaining the public's trust. The second part was a bit more delicate—getting his estranged wife to quietly sign the annulment papers. The question that needed answering was why had she ignored the papers for months now?

By the time the revitalization project had finally gotten off the ground, so had Zoe's career as an interior designer. She'd worked on some of the most notable buildings here in Bellacitta, the capital of Mirraccino. With the public enthralled with her work, he knew he needed to hire her. His advisors, knowing his history with Zoe, said he was foolish. But Demetrius insisted he had reasons for this unorthodox approach.

His first reason was that she had a flare with colors and arrangements—a way to make people sit up and take notice without it being over-the-top. And the second reason was to be able to get close to her without arousing the press's suspicions. With her close at hand, he'd be able to work the answers out of her that he needed to put his short-lived marriage to a very quiet end.

Demetrius struggled to maintain his calm and easy demeanor. "Today, I'd like to focus on Mirraccino and in particular the South Shore redevelopment. It's very important to me and to the king. It promises to bring new homes and businesses to the area as well as create new job opportunities for the local residents."

"So the rumors of a new princess are false?"

Drawing on a lifetime of experience of dealing with the media, he spoke in a calm, measured tone. "You will be my first call when I have a marriage announcement. But I believe right now the viewers would like to hear more about the project."

The reporter's brows rose and her eyes filled with unspoken questions, but he met her gaze head-on. If she dared to continue this line of questioning into his personal life, he'd wrap up this interview immediately. It wasn't as if she was the only reporter on the island, though she did host the nation's most popular entertainment show.

Color infused her cheeks as she at last glanced at the camera. "The South Shore project is going to benefit quite a number of people. How exactly did you come up with the idea to revitalize this area?"

"This endeavor is something that has been of interest to the crown for some time now. However, it wasn't until recently that we were able to gain the last of the property deeds in order to push ahead with the plans."

The loud rumble of an engine caught his attention. He sought out the source of the noise. It was a taxi that had pulled to the curb near his limo. A tall, willowy brunette emerged from the blue-and-white taxi. She turned and leaned in the passenger window as she handed over the cab fare. If Demetrius didn't know better, he'd swear that was his wife. But he refused to let his imagination get the best of him and upend this interview.

He turned back to Ms. Russo. "Residenza del Rosa is our first project. We will have it up and running by the beginning of the new year."

"So you have plans for more than just the mansion?" Ms. Russo sent him an expectant look.

"*Sì.*" Demetrius swallowed hard and forced his thoughts back to business. "Residenza del Rosa is already well underway. As soon as we have the necessary funding secured, we will start on phase two, which will be to build affordable housing." The clicking of heels caught his attention. He refused to be distracted. Security would handle it. "We intend to make the South Shore accessible to both the young and the young at heart. This area will once again be a robust community."

The head of his security detail approached him. Demetrius held up a finger to pause the interview. The bodyguard leaned over and whispered in his ear. "It's a Ms. Sarris. She has a pass and she says she works here. Should we let her through?"

"Oh, look." Ms. Russo's face lit up. Too late. She'd caught sight of Zoe. The reporter's eyes sparkled as though she'd been given a special treat. "Isn't that the interior designer, Zoe Sarris?"

Before answering the reporter, Demetrius gave an affirmative yet reluctant nod to his man to allow Zoe to join them. That woman certainly did have bad timing—first when she walked out on him just hours after saying "I do"—and now. How did she do it?

He could feel the reporter's gaze on him. He cleared his throat. "Yes, it's Miss Sarris."

"I wonder what she's doing here?" The reporter sent him a speculative look. "Did you arrange this?"

He resisted the urge to frown at the reporter's fishing expedition as well as the fact that his estranged wife was about to crash his very important interview. "No. It appears she's here to work. We've been lucky enough to obtain Ms. Sarris's exclusive services to create a welcoming yet relaxing environment for the future residents of Residenza del Rosa."

"And what features will it provide?"

"This long-term care home will be able to accommodate different levels of care from assisted living to skilled nursing."

"And Ms. Sarris is here to make this mansion into the beauty it once was?"

"We're hoping she'll be able to take what is here and give it a fresh feel."

"I'm sure she will. Is Miss Sarris signed on for the other buildings in the revitalization project?"

"Not at this point. We want to see how this first building goes and then we'll reevaluate, figuring out what works and what doesn't."

Ms. Russo nodded in understanding. "How splendid that she can join us and give our viewers an idea of what she has in mind for the place. I've seen her work before and it's fantastic. In fact, we can do before and after shoots of the mansion, both inside and out, with your permission of course."

"That sounds like a good idea."

Demetrius followed Ms. Russo's gaze to the woman in question. Zoe's clothing choice was nothing out of the ordinary, a short black skirt and a pink blouse. But on her, it looked fantastic as it nestled her curves perfectly—curves that he still knew by memory. She lifted her black sunglasses and then shook out her long dark curls before resting her shades atop her head like a hairband.

No matter what had gone down between them, there was

no denying the obvious—she was a knockout. He should glance away—check his phone—continue the interview— anything but continue to stare at her.

Her legs were long, toned and tan. He couldn't have turned away even if he'd have tried, which he had no inclination to do. It'd been months since he'd laid eyes on her. Visions of her in his dreams didn't count—they couldn't hold a candle to the real thing.

Zoe moved one strappy black high heel in front of the other. The classic ZZ Top song "Legs" started playing in his head. This girl definitely knew her strongest attributes and she worked them—no wonder he'd fallen for her hard and fast. Was it possible that she was even more gorgeous now than she had been when they'd met more than a year ago?

"It's warm standing here in the sun. Perhaps we should move to the shade." Ms. Russo signaled to her cameraman to take a break. "Prince Demetrius, are you all right?"

The concern in the reporter's voice startled him out of the trance he'd fallen under. He drew a breath of air into his straining lungs. With effort, he turned his gaze from Zoe to the reporter who wore an inquisitive expression.

Not good, Demetrius. Not good at all. Stay focused.

He cleared his throat. "Sorry. I just remembered something that needs my attention. Let me just make a note of it." He pulled out his phone and made the pretense of typing something while he got his brain screwed on straight.

The same question kept playing over and over in his mind. What in the world was Zoe doing here? Surely she hadn't come to see him. No. That was impossible. His schedule was kept under wraps for security purposes. Even Ms. Russo had not been alerted to the location for this interview until this morning. So that still left the question of why Zoe had crashed this important interview?

Demetrius slipped his phone back in his jacket pocket. "Okay. Where were we?"

"I thought we might want to wait for Ms. Sarris to join us."

Her comment had him instinctively turning back to the woman who'd gained the reporter's attention. Zoe climbed the last two steps in those sky-high black heels that made her legs look as though they went on and on forever. His mouth grew dry and his palms became moist.

He should have had his men turn her away. How was he supposed to concentrate on the interview when all he wanted to do was confront Zoe?

He only had one question: Why?

Okay. So maybe he did have a couple more questions. Like, when did she start dressing like that? Were her skirts always so short? How was a man to make intelligent conversation when all he could think about was her bare, tanned legs?

Concentrate on the business at hand.

Every muscle in his body tensed. He couldn't continue to stare at her. He didn't want anyone to notice that he was affected by Zoe's presence.

"Excuse me." Zoe's gaze didn't quite meet his. "I didn't know anyone would be here today. If it's okay, I'll just go inside and make some notes."

"No problem." Demetrius backed up to let her pass by.

"Wait." Ms. Russo stepped in Zoe's way. "Ms. Sarris, would you have a couple of minutes to speak with us?"

Zoe shook her head. "I don't want to intrude."

"You aren't. In fact, I'd like to get a few quotes from you. But first I need to go track down my cameraman. He wanted to film a few frames of the mansion under construction."

Demetrius waited until the reporter was out of earshot before turning to Zoe. "What are you doing here?"

"I already told you. I came to take notes." Her steady gaze met his. "What are you doing here?"

Leave it to Zoe to question a prince. She never was one to be awed by someone's position or power. To her, everyone put on their pants one leg at a time just like everyone else. Then again, that was one of the things he'd always admired about her. But suddenly, it wasn't so admirable—suddenly she made him uncomfortable having to explain himself.

Though his family thought he'd only known Zoe for a few weeks, the truth was that they'd been involved for six months before taking the plunge. When his family found out about their elopement, chaos had ensued, so he never got a chance to correct them. Besides, what difference would it have made? His family had already determined that he was impulsive and foolish to rush into marriage with someone so unfitting for the role of princess.

But that was then and things had changed a lot since then. Now Demetrius was cautious and he thought out his actions before he acted. In fact, he'd planned out what he would say to Zoe when they first met up again, but he hadn't expected it to be here on these steps—in public—in front of a television camera.

Not about to get into anything personal right now, he settled on, "I'm the prince and I have every right to be here. After all, this project is under the direct supervision of the Crown."

"Of course." Her cheeks took on a pink tinge. "I should have known. I was just caught off guard by your presence."

"Listen, there's something you should know—"

"Sorry about that." Ms. Russo smiled as she rejoined them.

Demetrius cleared his throat. It was time to put this all to an end before it blew up in his face. Instead of gaining the public's trust, he might just damage his reputation beyond repair if they unearthed the truth about his very brief, very rushed marriage.

Demetrius stepped forward. "Ms. Sarris just informed me that she won't be able to stay."

CHAPTER TWO

So much for thinking Christmas had come early.

There appeared to be a lump of coal in her stocking.

Zoe arched a brow at Demetrius. Question after question crowded her mind. Like what exactly was her ex-husband really up to? Then again, their marriage had been annulled so technically he wasn't her ex. So what did that make him? Her fairy-tale past? Her delicious mistake?

Not that any of it mattered.

They were history. That part was undeniable.

"The prince is correct. I just stopped by to check on something." Zoe made sure to wear her friendliest smile. "If you'll excuse me."

She stepped past Demetrius and kept walking. The murmur of their voices resumed. It wasn't until she'd reached the other end of the landing that she paused and glanced over her shoulder.

Her gaze scanned over Demetrius's tailored charcoal-gray suit and polished dress shoes. He looked quite smart in his designer clothes. His hair was a little shorter and styled. So much for the laid-back, not-worried-about-his-looks prince. The tide had most definitely turned. The man standing in front of the camera definitely had a serious persona about him.

What had happened to turn Demetrius into the focused prince standing before her? The question teetered on the tip of her tongue, but she knew that it was no longer any of her business. The thought settled as a lump in her stomach. She'd done what she thought was best at the time by walking away—even if she had loved him.

When his dark gaze met hers, the breath hitched in her throat. It was abundantly clear that she was the very last person he'd expected to see today. And he was none too happy about it. Her fingers fidgeted with the material of her skirt. Would he have her replaced?

Zoe's stomach dipped. This job was not only impressive but it also paid well—quite well. It'd certainly improve her declining bank account and give her the funds necessary to continue helping her ailing mother. Without it, she didn't know how she'd make do.

She'd lingered too long. It was time to slip inside the mansion away from the paparazzi, away from the questions—away from Demetrius's accusing stare. She was just about at the front door of the mansion when a man stepped out from behind one of the columns.

"Smile for the camera, sweetie." He snapped a picture of her.

The flash momentarily blinded her. She stood rooted in the same spot. What in the world?

The man was short and had a paunch. He hadn't seen a razor recently and his hair was greasy with a long, stringy comb-over. His eyes narrowed in on her. "They're going to love you."

"Who are you? What do you want?"

"I'm the man who's going to learn your secrets."

There was no way he was with Ms. Russo. Zoe started to back up. Not realizing there was a step behind her, she tripped and a scream tore from her lungs.

"Zoe?" Demetrius called out.

Her hands flailed about as she struggled to regain her balance. And then suddenly there was a steadying hand clutching her arm, pulling her to safety. Once she was on level footing, her gaze met Demetrius's concerned look.

"Are you all right?" His voice was gruff with concern.

"I'm fine." She glanced around but the man who'd startled her was gone.

"Did you see that man?"

Demetrius shook his head. "Was it one of the construction workers?"

"I don't think so. He had a camera."

Demetrius called over one of his security detail, and in hushed tones they spoke. Then he turned back to her. "Don't worry. If he's still here, they'll find him. Do you know what he wanted?"

Zoe shook her head.

Ms. Russo rushed over. "Is everything okay?"

"There was a man here," Demetrius explained. "He startled Miss Sarris."

The reporter lowered her microphone. "I caught a glimpse of him just as he turned to leave."

Zoe was so relieved to know that someone had seen him. "Do you know who he is?"

"I don't know his name." Ms. Russo's dark brows drew together. "I've seen him before. I think he may be a stringer, selling whatever dirt he digs up on celebrities to the highest paying publication. He doesn't look it, but he's very good at sniffing out the scandalous stories." Ms. Russo's gaze moved from Zoe to Demetrius. "So Prince Demetrius, do you know why he's investigating you?"

Demetrius frowned. "I have no idea."

Wanting to diffuse this line of questioning, Zoe spoke up. "What will happen if they catch him?"

Demetrius's gaze met hers. "Did he hurt you?" When she shook her head, he continued. "He'll most likely be questioned and released."

It wasn't exactly a comforting thought to know that man would soon be loose. But Demetrius was right. They couldn't lock him up just because he'd scared her.

"Don't look so worried." Demetrius's voice was low and comforting. "He was interested in me, not you."

Zoe wasn't so sure about that. The man's beady eyes had been staring right at her when he'd spoken. Goose bumps raced down her arms. She'd prefer to never see him again.

"Are you all right?" The reporter sent her a worried look.

Zoe nodded. "I should be going."

"Please don't rush off." Ms. Russo gestured to her cameraman to start filming. "Since you're here, can you give us some idea of what to look forward to with the mansion?"

Zoe wanted to leave—to get as far away as fast as possible. But how would that look? Talk about giving credence to that creep's allegations that she had secrets. She refused to let him or anyone else run her off.

With every bit of willpower she could muster, Zoe flashed the camera a smile. "Sure. As long as Prince Demetrius doesn't mind."

He made a pretense of checking his Rolex watch. "I suppose we have time. But it will have to be quick. I have another meeting shortly."

"Certainly." The reporter's eyes gleamed with victory.

The woman started rambling off questions about the project as the cameraman filmed the whole session. It was bad enough running into her ex, but now to be filmed with him for primetime television made her want to groan. Could this day get any worse?

"Now, how did you two meet?"

"What?" When all three people turned inquisitive eyes Zoe's way, the heat of embarrassment inched up her neck. "Sorry." She searched for the easiest way out of this mess. "I got distracted. What did you ask?"

"I was wondering how you and the prince met."

Zoe waited, hoping Demetrius would speak up and put an end to this interview. But instead he remained silent, letting the awkward silence grow. Zoe improvised. "We don't really know each other."

The reporter's brow arched. "That's interesting. I'd have sworn you two seemed to know each other. Are you sure there wasn't another project? Or a social engagement?"

"We don't move in the same social circles," Zoe said with utter honesty.

At last, Demetrius found his voice. "This is actually our first project together and Miss Sarris might not remember, but we met ever so briefly at the opening of the DiCapria corporate offices. She'd done such an excellent job with its design that when the Residenza del Rosa project came up, her name immediately came to mind."

Of course Zoe remembered that moment. It had been the night her whole world changed. So then how could he just stand there and talk about their very first meeting at the DiCapria party as though nothing had come of it? It had been the precipice of her heart tumbling and careening into his.

"The DiCapria office is beautiful." Ms. Russo turned to her. "That project brought you a lot of public attention. Would you say it was a turning point in your career?"

"Definitely." Zoe was very proud of that project. They'd given her a lot of freedom with the design and she'd ended up impressing everyone. "It was and still is one of my favorite projects."

"I'll make a note to get some photos of the DiCapria offices to include in this exposé." The woman keyed a note into her phone. "And if we could just have one more photo of you two together for our website, we'll be done."

Zoe's cheeks ached from smiling so much. *Don't they already have enough footage?* But when she glanced up the cameraman had gone to exchange his filming equipment for a digital camera.

While the reporter spoke to the camera guy, Demetrius

leaned close and spoke in her ear. "Hang in there. Doing what she asks will be a lot faster and easier than trying to duck out."

His crisp, fresh cologne teased her memory. She remembered all too clearly what it was like to lean into him and press her mouth to the smooth skin of his neck. His quickening pulse would thump beneath her lips as she'd leave a trail of kisses from his jaw down to his chest—

She groaned as she drew her thoughts up short.

That was then. This is now.

Demetrius sent Zoe a warning look as her groan reached his ears.

She had to hang in there just a little longer.

This interview couldn't fall apart now.

If he failed to gain the nation's confidence, there was a very good chance that anarchy would ravage this very beautiful island nation his father had spent his whole life protecting. Demetrius would do all he could to keep that from ever happening to his much-loved homeland.

Most of all, he couldn't let down his father. He knew in the grand scheme of things that it shouldn't weigh so heavy on him, but his father hadn't had the easiest life despite his position. When Demetrius was fifteen, his mother had been murdered in an assassination attempt. It'd fractured their family.

His twin, Alexandro, blamed himself for the murder and had assumed the role of protector. Their father had grown quiet and reserved, spending all of his time working. Demetrius had gone a bit wild, living life to its fullest. He never thought any of them would be happy again.

Then last year, his brother had led the paparazzi on a wild chase to the United States to divert attention from Demetrius's elopement to Zoe. And his brother's daring plan had worked...sort of. While in the States, Alex had fallen in love and married an American. Somewhere during all of this, they'd started to act like a family again—sharing meals and catching up on each other's lives. And he couldn't lose that. Not again.

But now being here with Zoe, he realized he'd made a huge mistake by thinking they could work side by side. His gaze strayed to her. She was answering some more questions about her profession for the reporter.

His gaze skimmed down over her, noticing on closer inspection that her clothes hung a bit loose. Had she lost weight in the time they were apart? She had been slender when he knew her. The fact that she'd lost weight was worrying. He hoped she wasn't sick. He studied her face. She didn't look ill.

As he continued to stare at her, he felt the draw of attraction as strong now as it had been back when they were together. Was it possible she was even more beautiful today than she had been when he'd pledged his heart to her? His gaze slipped to her full lips—

Realizing the direction of his straying thoughts, he jerked them to a halt. No matter how tempting he still found her, he refused to fall for her charms again. His foolish behavior had already cost him so much.

"We're almost done." The reporter clasped her hands together. "I just need a couple more candid shots for the website. Could you both move to the edge of the steps?"

While they moved into the designated positions on the top step, he chanced another glance Zoe's way. Her lips lifted at the corners. However, her smile didn't quite reach her brown eyes. He wasn't about to complain. At least she was playing along.

"Can you shake hands?"

With anyone else, the request would have been simple, but Zoe was not just anyone. She was most definitely someone—someone he was over. His jaw tightened. So then why was he making such a big deal out of this?

He extended his hand to her.

There was a moment's hesitation. Her gaze met his, but he couldn't read what she was thinking. When her hand slipped into his, there was a jolt—no, it was more like a lightning bolt—of awareness that coursed between them.

It means nothing.

She means nothing.

It's all in my imagination.

"Hold that pose." The reporter turned and frowned at the camera guy. "What's the problem? Don't keep the prince waiting."

The photographer waved over the reporter. With a flustered look on Ms. Russo's face, she uttered an apology and rushed down the steps to straighten out the problem.

"Are you really planning to oversee this project personally?" Zoe's gaze was hard and cold.

He lowered his voice to a whisper. "Why wouldn't I? This is my project. Surely you know that."

"I know that they were bandying your name about when I was hired, but I figured they were just trying to impress me. I had no idea you could actually be persuaded to take part in this venture."

He wanted to take offense. He wanted to assure her that he was always on top of things. But then again, not so long ago, he'd had his priorities all turned around. Back then, he'd only been worried about his personal happiness. Even as a teenager, he'd known that once he stepped up and took his rightful place in the monarchy that his life would not be his own. So he'd put off the inevitable as long as possible.

He kept his voice low. "Things have changed since you knew me."

"You act like we were just strangers that passed in the night."

Demetrius cleared his throat. Using the same voice he used when his advisors didn't agree with him, he whispered, "This revitalization project is important. There's a whole lot more at stake than just my reputation—"

"Sorry about that." Ms. Russo joined them again. "My cameraman had a problem with the equipment. We need to film the part where you shake hands again." Hesitantly they joined hands while Ms. Russo smiled. "This is great! The viewers will love it. This will definitely add a sense of hands-on attention by the prince."

Hands-on. The words conjured up the memory of Zoe in his arms. Demetrius schooled his facial features to keep the unintended meaning of the reporter's words from showing. He didn't dare look at Zoe. He didn't want to do anything to bring about a reaction in her. After all, how was he supposed to smile and relax while standing next to the one woman that he thought he could trust above all others?

"Can you look at each other?"

Demetrius reluctantly gazed at Zoe. Her gaze was closed and guarded. She was none too excited about this unexpected reunion, either. Well, good, he was more than willing to share the discomfort, although it didn't come close to the agony he'd experience after she'd run out on him.

"Good. Good." The reporter's voice held a happy tone. Obviously she was the only one happy about this encounter. "Now could you continue to shake hands while talking about the project? We need a sound bite—one showing you two working together. A team effort."

Demetrius cleared his throat. "*Grazie*. Your presence is appreciated."

There was a pause and Demetrius tensed, waiting and wondering what Zoe would say.

"I'm honored to have been chosen for this very special project."

"We are the lucky ones to have your talent to create a

stunning retreat for the residents of this facility to forget about their lives—their problems—and just relax in the common rooms of this historic building."

There was the slightest flash of emotion in Zoe's eyes, but in a blink it was gone. "I hope to live up to your expectations."

He'd give her credit. She was keeping this professional. Then again, he could never fault Zoe for acting anything but mature and professional. Otherwise they'd have never been able to maintain a relationship that was out of sight of the paparazzi. Which left him with a question that had been nagging him since she'd left him—why hadn't she sold her story—their story—to the tabloids?

His gaze narrowed in on the woman standing before him. He didn't understand her any more now than he did before. Perhaps he understood her even less. His advisors had insisted she was holding out for a bigger payday— bigger than the check he'd insisted on sending with the annulment papers. Was that why she'd never signed and returned the papers?

He withdrew his hand and turned to the reporter. "Ms. Sarris needs to get on with her work."

Zoe thanked both of them and turned away. Then instead of leaving, she headed inside the building. The fact she didn't use the opportunity to make a hasty escape surprised him. Then again since the night she'd walked out on him, everything she did surprised him.

CHAPTER THREE

THIS CAN'T BE HAPPENING.

It must be some sort of nightmare.

Zoe seriously considered pinching herself, but before she could put her thought into action, she heard footsteps behind her. Her pencil paused over the rough sketch she'd been making of the ballroom with notes for a tentative design.

She didn't even have to turn around to know who was behind her. It was Demetrius. What did he want now? The sure, steady steps of his dress shoes clicked over the marble floor, growing louder as he grew nearer. The footsteps stopped. He cleared his throat as though to gain her attention. Her entire body tensed.

The truth of the matter was that she owed him an explanation. It was long overdue. But this was not the time nor the place for this reunion. She didn't even know what to say to him. "Sorry" just wasn't enough. Regardless, there was no chance of ignoring him.

She leveled her shoulders and turned. "Did you need something, Your Highness?"

"You can stop with the 'Highness' bit, we're alone."

Zoe's gaze darted around the room, just to be sure. She took a calming breath. "I honestly didn't expect to find you here."

"Obviously. Your start date isn't until tomorrow. What are you doing here early?"

The easiest solution would be for her to hand in her resignation here and now. The words teetered on the tip of her tongue. But the artistic part of her didn't want to walk away from this amazing opportunity. This mansion was steeped in Old World charm and beauty. However, her feet were poised to run from the one man in this world who could make her heart flutter with excitement with just one dark, mysterious gaze.

Fight or flight? Fight or flight?

Her spine stiffened and her chin lifted. "I wanted to be prepared for tomorrow when I meet with Mr. Belmonte."

"Your meeting isn't with him."

"What do you mean?"

"I mean that your meeting is with me. I requested you for this job."

Zoe's stomach lurched. None of this made any sense. Why would he hire her with their messy history?

"By the time this job is completed, this mansion is going to be restored to its former glory. It'll start outside with the sweeping steps and the large, white columns and continue inside with its vintage style. In this section, I want people to forget that it's a care home and instead feel as though they've been transported to a tranquil place. Do you think you can deliver something like that?"

She glanced around at the peeling paint and the chipped plaster. The mansion had been downright neglected. It was hard to imagine the building being transformed into one of beauty. But she knew that it could be done.

"Of course I can do it." Her unwavering gaze met his. "But you knew that or you wouldn't have hired me."

"True enough."

"What are you really up to? And don't tell me that you hired me out of the goodness of your heart. I won't believe you."

Demetrius's dark brows rose. "If I didn't know better, I'd swear you just implied that I'm heartless."

"I don't want to play word games with you." She took a

second to pull herself together, because it felt as though her world had just slipped off its axis. "What are you up to?"

"I would think that is obvious. This is a royal project and I am overseeing it from start to finish."

"Not that. I want to know why you hired me of all people."

"Does it matter?"

"It does." There was something more—something he wasn't saying.

The man standing before her wasn't the same man she'd married—the man who'd swept her off her feet was sweet and fun. His biggest worry back then had been wondering what he'd do for entertainment the next day. She didn't understand how someone in his position could have lived his life so carefree, but obviously it'd all caught up with him. Because this man with his lips pressed together into an uncompromising line while staring directly at her meant business—of that she was certain.

He crossed his muscular arms. "Perhaps hiring you was a mistake—"

"No—" She bit back her next words but it was too late. Demetrius's brows lifted at her sudden outburst. "I mean, we have an agreement. Or at least I do with Mr. Belmonte."

"Agreements are made to be broken."

"But it's in writing."

"And you didn't think that I would leave myself a loophole—a way out if the need arose?"

Who is this man? And what had happened to the laidback Demetrius?

Her gut told her to get out now. That she was getting in far too deep with a man who still had a hold on her heart. But what kind of daughter would that make her? This was her chance to make the remainder of her mother's life better.

And to complicate matters further, she had no job to return to. She'd already resigned from her position as interior designer for the island's most prominent and discriminating furniture store. And most important, this job paid well—well enough to pay her mother's bills.

Zoe was stuck.

"You still haven't answered my question. Why did you hire me?" She watched him carefully, not sure what sort of reaction to expect.

"I wanted the best for this job. And you are the best on the island."

Was he serious? He thought she was the best? A warmth swirled in her chest and rose to warm her cheeks. Their gazes connected and held. Her heart thudded harder, faster. She refused to acknowledge that his words meant anything to her. She was over him. Past him.

"So you just expect us to work together like…like nothing ever happened?"

A loud bang echoed through the expansive ballroom.

Demetrius's body tensed.

"What was that?" Zoe whispered.

He didn't know but he certainly intended to find out. He peered around the various drop cloths, plaster buckets and scaffolding. "Who's there?"

A movement caught his attention. Across the room, a worker in a yellow hard hat straightened from where he'd dropped a load of lumber. He glanced their way. "Hey, you aren't supposed to be in here. This is a designated hard hat area."

Demetrius nodded his understanding. "We were just leaving."

"See that you do. I don't want to have to throw you out." The man turned and walked away.

Obviously the man hadn't recognized him with the shadows and the distance. That was all right with Demetrius. Sometimes he got tired of being the prince, of posing for pictures and answering questions. Sometimes he just wanted to be plain old Demetrius. He'd been able to pull that off not so long ago when he was partying and showing up in places most inappropriate for royalty. But those times were over and not to be repeated.

Zoe laughed. The sound startled him. It'd been so long since he'd seen her happy. In the beginning, their relationship had been an easy and relaxed one. He missed those times. He hadn't relaxed like that since—

No. He wasn't going down memory lane. That was then. This is now.

Everything had changed over the past year. He refused to be swayed by the way the gold specks in her eyes twinkled when she smiled or how her cheeks filled with color when she was paid a compliment. He was immune to it all.

Zoe turned her attention back to him. "I guess he didn't realize who he was threatening to toss out of here."

"The man was just doing his job and making sure that no one is injured on his watch."

"Then I guess we better hurry." She turned and snapped a couple more pictures of the room with her phone. "I've already been given the dimensions of the rooms as well as the architectural drawings." She glanced around again. "And now with these photos, I should be able to get started. We should get going before that man comes back."

Demetrius stepped in front of her. "Not so fast. We need to establish guidelines for our working arrangement."

"That's easy. When I have some sketches, I'll contact you."

When she once again started around him, he reached out and grasped her wrist. "That won't work. I want a more hands-on approach."

She yanked her arm away and glared at him. "Surely you aren't proposing to look over my shoulder?"

"That's not how I would have worded it, but so be it."

Zoe planted her hands on her hips. "I don't work well under close supervision. I need room to do my research and then I start sketching and playing with colors. It isn't going to be an overnight project. It will take me time."

"I understand that. As long as you understand that you'll need to keep your design plans a secret from everyone— even your family and friends. The big reveal will be the week of the Royal Christmas Ball. Large contributors will be invited to wow them into donating more funding for more renovations in the neighborhood. The following day, Ms. Russo will be airing another segment on her television show giving viewers before and after shots of the mansion."

Zoe nodded her understanding. "Trust me. No one will see my designs. When I have something ready for you to see, we can meet in the village at the *caffè* house."

"That's impossible. My daily presence in the village, as well as the security detail, would be far too disruptive to businesses."

A frown pulled at her beautiful face. "Fine. What do you suggest?"

Demetrius glanced over, noticing the workman had yet to return, but his gut told him the man would be back soon. They had to make this brief. "I think our best solution is to work at the palace."

"The palace?" Zoe's face noticeably paled.

"Offices have been set up there for the architect, the PR consultant and others. It will be very handy having all of the key people under one roof."

"But I don't have a car."

He hadn't thought of that, but if that was her only objection, he'd find a solution. "I'll send my car for you."

Her mouth opened, but then she closed it as though she'd run out of protests.

Good. Another problem solved. "Now that we have that

straightened out, let's get out of here before that guy comes back. I don't relish the idea of facing him down."

The worry lines smoothed on Zoe's face. "You don't have anything to worry about. I remember how you'd visit the gym each morning, not to mention your evening run along the beach. I'm guessing you still do both."

"I do. When time allows." Demetrius's shoulders straightened. Had she just paid him a compliment? "Still, I prefer to keep a low-key presence."

"Since when? You used to love to be the playboy and you didn't care who photographed you."

"Things certainly have changed since those days."

She glanced away. "I guess they have."

Everything had changed, apparently for both of them. And the more time he spent with her, the more he wondered about those dark smudges under her eyes that her makeup didn't quite cover. Something was keeping her up at night. But what?

CHAPTER FOUR

WHAT HAD SHE been thinking?

Agreeing to work side by side with her ex.

And at the royal palace of all places.

The next morning, Zoe muttered to herself as she tried on outfit after outfit. The pile of discarded clothes on her bed was growing. What did one wear to the palace? Business attire? Nah, too stiff. A summer dress? Too casual. Nothing seemed fitting for the occasion.

And then she recalled that she wasn't an invited guest. She was the help. She'd probably be ushered in the back entrance and kept out of sight. With that in mind, she dressed as she normally would for a consultation—a short purple skirt, a white blouse and a pair of heels.

Up until now, she'd carefully avoided Demetrius. In some ways, it seemed like forever since that horrible day at the palace when her whole house of cards had come tumbling down, and in other ways it seemed like just the other day. Demetrius had no idea how much that decision had cost her—she'd sacrificed her heart that night. And her life had never been the same since then.

Leaving had been the only way she'd known to care for her mother and to protect the prince. With Zoe gone from his life, he could move on. He could find someone else to be his perfect princess—someone whose DNA didn't have a fifty-fifty chance of inheriting the blueprint for early onset familial Alzheimer's disease.

In the beginning, she'd let herself get so caught up in his attention—in the belief that their love could overcome anything. In the end, she'd learned the harsh reality of life.

Love couldn't fix everything.

If it could, her mother wouldn't be ill. Her mother wouldn't be fading away right before her very eyes.

As it was, her mother had just gone to stay with a family friend who had a house by the sea—the community where her mother had grown up. Her mother insisted that she wanted to go. She'd referred to it as her final vacation as the sea had always brought her mother great peace. The trip couldn't have come at a better time. It provided Zoe with a chance to make the most of this amazing opportunity.

The buzz of her phone drew Zoe out of her thoughts. The number was blocked. She could only figure that it must be the driver sent to pick her up. She stabbed her finger at the keypad and an unfamiliar male voice came over the line. It was indeed the driver. He was waiting for her in the back alley. It was obvious Demetrius didn't want to draw attention to her comings and goings. That was fine with her.

Most people in the building walked to work, making it possible for her to slip down the back stairs unnoticed. She entered the alley to find an unmarked black sedan with heavily tinted windows.

The driver opened the door for her. She climbed inside and leaned back against the cool leather seat. It was hard to believe that once upon a time this lifestyle had been hers. Sure it'd been brief—quite brief. But for a moment, it had been magical.

As the sedan rolled through downtown Bellacitta, she stared out at the colorful city. Though it was only November, the shops were already decked out in festive red and silver decorations. The lampposts were adorned with colorful wreaths. A sense of kindness and compassion was in the air. Zoe and her mother had always enjoyed this time of the year. Any other year, their Christmas tree would already be trimmed, supplies would be on hand for Christmas cookies and carols would fill their home.

A deep sadness filled Zoe because the Christmases she once knew were now nothing more than memories, and the future looked bleak.

When the car rolled to a stop at an intersection, Zoe got the strangest feeling that someone was staring at her. She glanced out the window. She didn't see anyone at first. Then at last her gaze rested on a man—the creepy reporter from the mansion. She froze.

He was standing on the sidewalk not more than a few feet away. He was staring at her. His dark eyes narrowed. Heavy scruff covered his squared jaw as his thin lips pressed into an unyielding line. The little hairs on Zoe's arms lifted. When he raised his camera, Zoe ducked back in her seat before realizing that the dark tint on the windows would shield her. It wasn't until the car was in motion again that she let out a pent-up breath. She rubbed her arms, easing away the goose bumps. At least she was going someplace he wouldn't be able to follow—of that she was certain.

As the car exited the city, she wondered what the reporter was after—something specific or was he just digging for a juicy nugget. She told herself to relax. Sooner or later, the man would give up and move on to another story. She just hoped it was sooner rather than later.

Zoe glanced out the window as they passed by the outskirts of the historic village of Portolino with it stone walkways, quaint shops and renowned craftsmen. It was a much slower pace than the city life of Bellacitta, but it held its own charms. Caught up in the throes of life, she hadn't been there since she was a child. If there was time someday after work, she wanted to visit the village, but the only way to do that was on foot. She'd have to remember to bring more sensible footwear.

The car slowed as it made a right turn. They wound their way along the long palace drive with its colorful foliage and the shadows of the palm trees. The last time she'd been driven up this driveway, it had been under the guise of moonlight. Today the sunshine was bright and cheery. This time it felt so different. Good in some ways. But then she glanced to her right, noticing the empty seat next to her. And not so good in other ways.

When the enormity of the palace came into view, the breath caught in her throat. Sure, she'd seen pictures of it all her life, but with it being tucked back in away from public view, she'd never had an opportunity to view it in the daylight. It was so impressive—reminding her once again that Demetrius didn't come from the same world as her.

She sat up straighter, taking in the palace's warm tan, coral and turquoise tones. The place was simply stunning. The palace's subtle curves and colorful turrets reflected an island flair that was Mirraccino. Sure the island nation had evolved with technology and such, but they also kept with traditions as much as possible. And she loved that Demetrius wanted that Old World feel for the mansion.

To her utter surprise, the car rolled to a stop at the front entrance. An enormous wooden door with brass fixtures swung open. An older gentleman in a black-and-white tux strode toward the car. She was so struck by this surreal moment as he opened the door for her that she failed to move. She'd never expected to be welcomed back here after things had ended badly between her and Demetrius. And though they weren't rolling out the red carpet for her, this was more than she'd ever imagined.

The butler stood aside. "Welcome, Miss Sarris."

Coming to her senses, she stood. "You were expecting me?"

The man nodded. "Prince Demetrius asked that you be escorted to the suite of offices reserved for the South Shore project. He said to tell you that he has been delayed, but he will catch up with you shortly."

She tried to ignore the disappointment that consumed her. It wasn't like Demetrius had invited her to the palace to relive the good old days. No, this was business, pure and simple. Then again, nothing was simple when it came to her ex—nothing at all.

She was guided inside where her heels clicked on the marble floor of the spacious entryway. The sound reverberated off the ornate walls and high ceiling. There were a couple of ladders and a tall pencil Christmas tree. Boxes of decorations littered the floor. It appeared she and her mother weren't the only ones to decorate early.

Zoe would have loved a bit of time to look around, but she was briskly ushered away—down a long hallway, around a corner and down a flight of steps. They turned another corner where the palace sprang to life in a flurry of activity. There were people holding electronic tablets, *caffè* cups and papers, hustling through the hallway. Everyone smiled and greeted her. They were definitely a very friendly bunch.

A smile tugged at Zoe's lips. Maybe this working arrangement wouldn't be so bad, after all. Especially if Demetrius was off attending to his princely duties. In that moment, she realized she'd been worried about nothing. As busy as this place was, she doubted she'd see Demetrius much at all.

"You'll be working in here." The butler stood aside to let her enter.

"Grazie."

"You are welcome, ma'am. I'm sure someone will be along to answer any questions you might have. Do you need anything before I go?"

She shook her head. "No."

"Very well, ma'am."

Alone in the room, she glanced around impressed by the enormity of it. The walls were painted a warm cream white. Detailed crown molding framed the ornate ceiling with a crystal chandelier. This was all for her?

She'd never been in an office so steeped in history. She glanced at one of the garden paintings on the wall. She'd bet it was older than her and worth far more than she earned in an entire year.

"You must be Zoe," came a young female voice.

Zoe spun around to find a pretty blonde standing in the doorway, wearing a friendly smile. "Hi. That's me. Did you ever see an office like this? It's amazing."

"I guess so if you like old stuff."

Old stuff? Try antiques. Heirlooms. Rare treasures. "Are you part of the palace staff?"

The young woman shook her head and her bobbed hair swished around her chin. "I was hired to work on the South Shore project." She stepped farther into the room. "My name's Annabelle."

"Nice to meet you. Looks like we'll be working together."

"I'm looking forward to it. If you have any questions, feel free to ask. I probably won't know the answer, but I'll be able to point you toward the right person to ask."

"You're here. Good." Both women turned at the sound of Demetrius's voice.

"I'll let you get to work." Annabelle made a hasty exit.

Zoe wished she could follow her new friend. Suddenly, this very spacious office seemed to shrink considerably. Thankfully Demetrius appeared to be a very busy man. So once he welcomed her, he'd be off to another meeting, she hoped.

Demetrius cleared his throat. "Sorry I'm late. I didn't mean to intrude."

"You didn't." She couldn't help but notice he looked immaculate with his short hair combed into submission and his tailored suit hugging his muscled shoulders and broad chest. Her heart kicked up its pace a notch or two. She assured herself that it was nothing more than nervousness. She swallowed hard. "We were just introducing ourselves. Annabelle seems really nice."

Demetrius's brows rose as though her admission caught him by surprise. "Annabelle's great. She's the daughter of the Duke of Halencia."

The news that Annabelle was an aristocrat dampened Zoe's excitement over having an ally behind the palace walls. For some reason she'd been thinking her newfound friend was just like her—a commoner.

"I'm surprised she'd want to work here." Zoe uttered her thoughts without realizing how it might sound.

Demetrius cleared his throat. "It's an arrangement between the duke and my father."

An arrangement? Could it be a marriage arrangement? Jealousy swift and sharp stabbed at Zoe's heart making the breath catch in her throat. Not that she had any right to feel anything about Demetrius moving on with his life. Now that their marriage had been annulled—erased—wiped clean—he was free to do as he pleased. This is what she wanted, wasn't it?

Forcing herself to act as though this bit of news didn't bother her, Zoe said, "I look forward to working with her."

"Good." He walked over to the larger of the two desks. When he noticed that she'd followed him, he stopped and turned. "Um. This is my desk. Yours is over there."

"You mean we're sharing an office?"

His dark brows rose. "Is that going to be a problem?"

The professional part of her knew the answer was supposed to be no, but her scarred heart said otherwise. It sounded like she had a frog in her throat when she choked out, "No. No problem at all."

A puzzled expression came over his face. "We ran out of offices. And with you being the newest member of the team, it was either fit you in here or move you to another wing by yourself."

She swallowed hard. "If I'm in your way, I don't mind working elsewhere."

He shook his head. "I'm hardly ever in here, so it won't be a problem."

She supposed his frequent absence was some small consolation.

Zoe moved to the other side of the room and settled her laptop and day planner on the desk where she noticed a vase of fresh cut flowers. Red, white and purple blossoms beckoned to her. She leaned forward and inhaled their perfumed scent.

All the while she could feel Demetrius's gaze following her every movement. She needed to show him—show herself—that she was over him. She could be just as professional as him—even if his mere presence could still make her stomach shiver.

She stepped around the desk and crossed the great divide. She stopped in front of his massive carved cherry desk and laced her fingers together.

He glanced up from his computer monitor. "Did you need something?"

"I wanted to thank you for this opportunity. I won't let you down." His eyes reflected a mixed reaction. Perhaps she could have worded it better. "I also wanted to tell you that I won't let the past come between us."

His dark brows drew together as he shushed her. With long, swift strides, he moved to the door. He noiselessly pushed it closed before turning back to her. "If I didn't think you could be professional, you wouldn't be here."

She didn't know whether to be complimented or insulted. "*Grazie*."

"As for the other matter, we do need to talk. We have some unresolved business to address. But I don't want to get into it here. It'd be too easy to be overheard. And I don't want rumors to start."

"Neither do I." But obviously for different reasons than him. "You don't have to worry, Annabelle won't hear anything about the past from me."

"I hope not. Now if you'll excuse me, I have a meeting with the contractor." And with that he swung open the door and set off down the hallway, leaving her to wonder what his cryptic comment had meant.

What unresolved business?

CHAPTER FIVE

"How's it coming?"

Demetrius strolled into the office late the next afternoon. He couldn't help but notice how Zoe jumped. He hadn't meant to startle her.

"Good." Her voice said otherwise. "Well, as good as can be expected at this stage."

"I just visited the work site and the construction of the residential rooms on the backside of the mansion is moving ahead of schedule. Soon you'll be able to get in there and do your thing."

A frown pulled at her full, lush lips, but she didn't say anything. Things definitely weren't going as well as she'd like him to believe. Maybe she wasn't up to the task, after all. There were still those dark smudges beneath her eyes. Something was most definitely keeping her up at night. But what?

His immediate instinct was to go to her—to rectify whatever was troubling her. He took a step forward, then hesitated. What was he thinking? Obviously he wasn't—at least not clearly. Her problems were no longer any of his concern. And that had been her choice. Not his.

She glanced up at him, peering over her laptop. "Did you need something else?"

He cleared his throat. "I'd like to see what direction you're taking the project."

Her mouth gaped, but nothing came out. He couldn't help but notice the pink gloss shimmering on her lips. His thoughts rolled back in time, remembering how her kisses were always sweeter than berries. His body stiffened. With determined effort he focused his mind back on the only thing that mattered—the only thing he could count on—work.

"Perhaps I could see what you've been able to do so far on the computer." His words eased the awkward silence.

"I…I don't have anything but some rough outlines."

"That's okay. It's just with all of my meetings, we haven't been able to talk much."

There was a rebuttal reflected in her eyes, but in a blink it was gone. With a shrug, she stood up. "Be my guest."

He wasn't sure by the stilted tone of her voice whether she would be open to his feedback or if she'd just give him lip service and then disregard his input. He wanted to believe they could set aside their differences in order to make this important project a success. They were, after all, both professionals.

He took a seat, surprised that she was doing all of her work on the small laptop when he'd provided her with a computer and a large-screen monitor, which was much easier on the eyes. Then he noticed that she had specialized software. He should have expected that, but he'd noticed how his thoughts became severely distracted around her.

She stood off to the side. "You have to realize that what you're looking at are some rough sketches. There are no details. I haven't had a chance to refine them."

"I understand."

She showed him how to navigate the software. As she leaned over his shoulder, he caught a whiff of her perfume. The alluring scent was the same as what she wore when they were together.

Concentrate on the pictures.

Minutes passed, and then she asked, "Well, what do you think?"

"I don't know." It was the truth.

"Don't tell me you hate all of the themes."

He flipped back and forth between the three layouts of the mansion's ballroom that she'd done up. The first screen cobbled together garden-themed pictures with lots of greens, pinks and yellows. The second screen contained images more in line with ancient Roman ruins utilizing the idea of the large columns on the front porch as well as adding some Greek and Roman statues. The last screen pulled together various Mediterranean aspects from the blues of the sea to the green of the palms.

"Say something. The suspense is torture."

He'd never seen her so anxious. Under different circumstances, he might have turned this into a bit of fun, but the time for teasing and light banter had long passed them by.

"They all have aspects that I really like." He flipped through the images once again. "Can you combine them?"

"What?" She moved to stand on the other side of the desk in order to face him. "You're not serious, are you? They're too different. It would be a mess."

He raked his fingers through his hair. "I never said that I was any good at decorating. That's what I have you for."

She crossed her arms and leveled a steady stare at him. "And you're the one who insisted that we work on this together. You went on and on about how you had to approve everything."

He got to his feet. "Fine. I pick the garden theme. Wait. No. The sea one."

She waited as though sensing he would change his mind yet again. "You're sure about the sea setting?"

He thought for a moment and then nodded. "I think it's the most relaxing of all them. If the residents aren't capable of making an outing to the seaside, then we can bring it to them."

"Okay. Then we need to pick out a color scheme." She pulled up a few color combinations. "I'd like to get some samples up on the walls as soon as possible to get a real feel for the shades before we commit to a color scheme."

However, as she leaned over his shoulder to type something in the computer, one of her barrel-roll curls landed on his shoulder. A driving need grew in him to wrap her silky strands around his finger. If he were to turn ever so slightly—if he were to reach out to her and draw her closer—she'd land in his lap.

As though in a trance, he reached out. His fingers slid down over the soft, smooth strands. What would it hurt to taste her sweetness again? He started at the end of her curl. His finger and thumb worked together wrapping her hair inch by inch around his digit.

Her surprised gaze met his. His heart pounded in his chest. But there was something more in her gaze. Interest. Excitement. Desire.

The fact that he could still turn her on sent the blood roaring through his veins, drowning out his common sense. Long-denied desire drove him onward. One thing that couldn't be denied was that they had chemistry. They should have a warning sign—combustible when mixed.

With each twist of her hair, her face moved closer. He would show her what she'd given up. He'd remind her that all of this could have been hers if only she'd believed in them—if only she'd loved him.

A noise in the hallway caused her to jump back. He reluctantly relinquished his hold on her hair, allowing her to straighten. He tried to tell himself that it was for the best, but a sense of regret churned in his gut.

He cleared his throat as he tried to remember where they'd left off. "What about this gray-blue color? I like it."

There was an unmistakable pause before Zoe spoke. "That is a bit dark and you have to realize the darker the shade, the smaller the space will appear. Why don't you see what you like on this page?" She adjusted the computer so that it displayed dozens of much lighter shades of blue. "Trust me. They'll appear darker on the wall."

This time instead of hovering, she stepped back, giving him space. Though he knew it was for the best, he missed that brief moment where they'd recaptured a bit of the past. He'd have to be more alert going forward. Things were already complicated enough between them.

For the next hour, they went over the various shades, mixing and matching. There was even a slick computer software program that let her slip the colors into the basic layout of the common rooms. It gave them a better idea of what it would look like in real life. But Zoe insisted there was nothing like seeing it in person with the natural light bouncing off the walls. He took her word for it. They agreed to wait until then to make the final decisions.

Two full days had passed. And she still had a job.

Zoe smiled.

This arrangement, though a bit bizarre working with her ex, just might work out in the end.

After a long day at the palace offices, Zoe had Demetrius's car drop her off at the market so she could pick up some food for dinner—not that she had much appetite these days. It seemed her stomach was forever filled with the sensation of a swarm of fluttering butterflies. She hoped a salad might pique her appetite.

Armed with fresh fruit, vegetables and some still-warm-from-the-oven bread, she walked toward her apartment. Ever since she'd left the market, something hadn't felt right. Zoe glanced over her shoulder.

Nothing out of the ordinary.

Still, the little hairs on Zoe's arms remained lifted.

She picked up her pace. At an intersection, she paused and glanced back. Her gaze met a set of dark, menacing eyes. The creepy reporter. Her heart lurched.

Though he didn't approach her, there was something threatening about the way he looked at her. There was no point calling for help. What would she say? He looked at her the wrong way?

The best thing she could do was keep moving. It wasn't much farther to her apartment. Hopefully she'd lose him. Her feet moved rapidly along the sidewalk. She refused to glance back again. She was making too much of seeing the reporter. Still, she recalled his eerie words about finding out her secrets. What secrets? About her mother? Demetrius?

Zoe rushed across the street. Her apartment building was in the next block. Though she'd promised herself she wouldn't, she paused and glanced back. The street was busy as people rushed home to their families. She didn't see any sign of the reporter. She breathed a sigh of relief. Perhaps it'd just been a coincidence.

Once safely in her apartment, she did something she didn't normally do—locked her door. She rushed to the kitchen window and peered out. She searched up the street. Nothing. Down the street. Nothing.

Get a grip. You're imagining things.

And then she saw him across the street. He emerged from between the buildings. The breath caught in her throat. He leaned back against the bakery and pointed his camera up at her. She ducked out of sight. Hastily, she closed the kitchen curtains.

What do I do now?

She rushed to put her groceries in the fridge, having lost any bit of hunger she may have had. She thought of calling Demetrius, but what would she say? Some guy was following her? Would Demetrius believe her? And after the way she'd walked out of their marriage, why should he care?

Knock. Knock.

Zoe jumped.

She moved to the window and peeked out. The reporter was gone.

Knock. Knock.

Or was he?

It was time they talked.

And Zoe had given him the perfect excuse.

Demetrius glanced down at her leather-bound day planner. She always had it close at hand, marking every meeting and deadline in it. She impressed him with her attention to detail. He knew that he could have left the planner on her desk till the morning, but he liked having an excuse to visit her at home—especially if her mother answered the door.

He'd knocked twice but still no one answered the door. That was strange. He'd thought he'd overheard her mention to Annabelle that she was planning to stay in and make a salad—not that he'd stuck around eavesdropping. Perhaps she'd decided it was easier to eat out. That would be just his luck.

Unwilling to give up the thought of seeing her—of finally gaining some answers about the annulment—he knocked one last time.

"Go away!"

What?

"Zoe? Open the door."

"If you don't leave, I'm calling the *polizia*."

The *polizia*?

What is going on?

"Zoe, it's me. Demetrius. Open up."

There was the sound of footsteps. Then a pause as he felt her gaze through the peephole. Followed by the click of the lock. At last the door swung open. A pale-faced Zoe stood there.

"I...I wasn't expecting you." Her gaze didn't quite reach his.

"Obviously. Who did you think I was?"

She shook her head and waved away his question. "It's nothing."

"It is quite obviously something. I insist you tell me." Her face was devoid of color. Her eyes were filled with worry. He wasn't leaving until he got to the bottom of what had her scared.

"Remember that reporter from the interview at the mansion? You know, the creepy one?"

He nodded, not liking the direction this conversation was going. "What did he do to you?"

She shook her head again. "Nothing."

"You look awfully worked up for nothing. Tell me and let me be the judge."

"It's just that he's been lurking around here, watching me and taking photos."

Demetrius's gut tightened. "And just now you thought he was knocking on your door?"

She shrugged.

"When's the last time you saw him?"

"He followed me home from the market. I…I saw him out the kitchen window, standing across the street. He tried to take my picture, but I think I ducked before he could."

Without waiting to be invited inside, Demetrius strode past Zoe toward the aforementioned window. This was his fault for thrusting her into the media spotlight. Now that she was working closely with him, the media would want to know everything about her. They would dissect her life, looking for a juicy piece of gossip.

Demetrius swept aside the curtain and peered out at the busy roadway. He didn't see anyone acting suspicious. "Do you still see him?"

She moved to his side and gazed out at the numerous faces. "No. He disappeared just before you arrived. That's why I thought you were him."

Demetrius let the curtain fall back into place. He glanced around, noticing the quietness. "Are you here alone?"

She nodded. "My mother is visiting a friend at the coast."

"Well, you can't stay here alone. Pack a bag. Tonight you're staying at the palace."

Her eyes grew round. "No, I can't. I won't."

Why was she being difficult? This was for her own welfare. "You can and you will. I'm not leaving you here."

"I'll be safe. I'll keep the door locked." Her lips pressed into a firm line as her gaze took a defiant gleam.

He wasn't going to let her have her way. Not this time. Not with her safety at stake. "Why are you being stubborn? It's not like I'm asking you to return to the palace as my wife."

Her chin lifted. "So far I've been lucky enough to avoid the king and his advisors. I won't be able to do that if I'm living there. And…and I don't want to deal with them. I didn't exactly leave on the best of terms."

Demetrius couldn't argue that point. The king's advisors were certain that she was a gold digger, but surprisingly the king had been quite reserved with his thoughts about Demetrius's failed marriage. Maybe his father thought that he'd suffered enough without adding an "I told you so."

Still, there had to be an alternative. A way to assure himself of her safety until the media set their sights on a new target. He rolled the options around in his mind.

"I have the perfect alternative." Why he hadn't thought of it in the first place was beyond him.

Her eyes widened with interest. "You do? What?"

"You'll see. It's not far from here."

CHAPTER SIX

JUST AS DEMETRIUS had promised, his chauffeured car ushered them past the palace gates, beyond the palace itself and down a narrow lane Zoe didn't even know existed. Unspoiled green foliage and wild flowers lined both sides of the roadway. They were heading far, far away from any curious eyes. It sure was a good thing that she knew Demetrius as well as she did. Otherwise, she would be wary of their isolated destination.

"Where are we going?" She turned to Demetrius as he continued to type response after response into his phone.

His fingers paused as he glanced out the window. "We're almost there."

"That doesn't tell me anything."

"Stop worrying. I'm certain you'll approve."

"And if I don't?"

There was a moment of silence. "Then we'll go back to your apartment."

She didn't believe it'd be that simple. Nothing was ever simple when it concerned this particular prince—this very sexy prince. "What's the catch?"

"There isn't one." When she arched a brow at him, he sighed. "You don't believe me?"

"Let's just say I know you well enough to expect you not to give up so easily."

Like when he'd proposed to her on a starlit night along the seashore. He refused to take any answer but her acceptance. Not that accepting a marriage proposal from a prince had been a hardship. In fact, in that moment, it had been quite the opposite.

Demetrius slipped his phone in his pocket. "There's no catch."

"I don't believe you."

Their gazes met and held as though in a struggle of wills. Demetrius was the first to turn away. "Before we go any further with this argument, see if this will calm your worries."

When she turned to the window, her gaze landed upon a beautiful white beach house. It was like something out of a glossy magazine. The door and some of the trim was done in a light teal. The appearance was refreshing and welcoming. Was this part of the royal estate?

"It's amazing."

"I'm glad you like it." A smile lifted his lips and eased the stress lines marring his face.

The car pulled to a stop and the driver got out to open her door for her. "If you want to go inside, ma'am, I'll bring in your luggage."

"*Grazie.*" She turned back as Demetrius alighted from the car. "Is there anyone here?"

He shook his head. "It's all yours for as long as you need."

Zoe made her way down the stone walkway, passing by a garden full of exotic foliage and blossoms from bright yellow and orange to pink and deep red. It was impossible not to fall in love with this place.

Anxious to see if the interior was as impressive as the exterior, she grasped the brass door handle and swung open the teal door. She stepped inside, greeted by a light-gray tiled foyer. The house had an open floor plan with a spacious kitchen that could be closed off by some teal shutters. The interior decor was of white walls and teal trim like the outside.

An abundance of open windows let the sea breeze filter through the house. She'd never been to such a charming place. When Demetrius said he'd take care of her, he hadn't been kidding. This was her idea of paradise.

She moved to the wall of windows facing the Mediterranean. It was absolutely gorgeous. It didn't matter how many times she looked out over the sea, she never tired of it. It would appear her mother wasn't the only one having a seaside holiday of sorts.

Zoe heard footsteps behind her. "You can just set the bags by the door. I'll get them—"

"Are you sure?"

That deep, rich voice sent a wave of delicious sensations coursing up her spine. It was most definitely not the driver. She spun around, finding Demetrius standing there holding her bags. "Sorry. I thought you were the driver."

"I hope you're not disappointed. I sent him away."

"What? But why?" Being alone with the one man who could send her heart pounding with just a look was not a good thing. "I mean, I'm sure you have work to do."

"I do. But first we have to talk."

Talk? About what? She got the distinct impression from his serious expression that she wasn't going to like what he had to say. Was he going to blame her for the nosy reporter sniffing around for gossip?

Demetrius cleared his throat. "But first, do you approve of your accommodations?"

"It's absolutely amazing." Zoe moved to his side and retrieved her luggage. She glanced up at him and her stomach quivered with excitement. They may no longer be a couple, but that didn't mean she was immune to his charms. "I owe you an apology. I should have realized that you would have the perfect place in mind. *Grazie*."

"You're welcome. It's the family's escape from the palace life. A place where we can just be ourselves without the constant expectations that go along with royal life."

"I feel safe here." She glanced all around. "I can already imagine that I'll be spending a lot of time out on the deck."

"I've spent many hours there. It's great for clearing your mind."

"I'm sure it is." Not anxious for the ominous talk, she said, "Well, I know you have things to do and I have to unpack, so I won't keep you."

"Not before we talk."

Something told her that this much-changed prince didn't normally have lapses in his schedule. Whatever he wanted to speak to her about must be important. Had something happened with the renovation?

She hoped not, for more than one reason. The South Shore revitalization project was a hard-fought-for and long-awaited improvement. And somehow, someway Zoe planned to get her mother a spot at the Residenza del Rosa. The doctor had warned that finding her mother appropriate accommodations needed to be a priority. The time for hesitating had passed.

Zoe set down her suitcase next to the couch. "What's the matter? Has something happened at the mansion?"

Demetrius's brows scrunched together. "Why would you think that?"

"It's your tone and…and your demeanor. You have something serious on you mind."

"You're right. I do. This conversation is long overdue."

Her stomach churned. She forced her gaze to meet his. "What conversation?"

Demetrius raked his fingers through his hair. "I've been waiting for you to say something about it, but I'm so tired of playing these games with you."

"What games? I haven't been playing any games with you."

"Sure you have. Why else wouldn't you have signed the annulment papers?"

The whites of her eyes widened and her mouth gaped. Was she really going to try and act surprised? What did she hope to gain by acting all innocent?

All of his pent-up frustration came rushing to the surface. "Don't look so shocked. I'm certain it comes as no surprise to you that we're still husband and wife."

"What? But...but that can't be."

"It can be when you don't sign and return the annulment papers."

"No, that isn't right." She pressed her fingers to her forehead as though she were trying to piece everything together.

Was she angling to garner his sympathy? Well, it wouldn't work this time. Demetrius's wounded pride refused to accept anything but a reasonable explanation. His ego hadn't just been pricked. It had been slashed to ribbons. This had to stop. And it had to stop here.

He was on a roll now and he couldn't stop. Not until she admitted what she wanted from him. Did she want more money? Or did she regret the way she'd trampled over their wedding vows on her way out the door? Did she want him back? The wondering and the not knowing had been nagging at him for months now. "Were you hoping for a bigger payday?"

"No!" Her gaze narrowed. "You know me better than that. I ripped up the check and mailed the papers back to you."

"I don't know what you did with the check or the papers, but I never received them."

Her eyes filled with confusion. "Then...then that means we're still married?"

He nodded. For the first time since the dreadful day when she walked out on him, he witnessed that same anguished look on her face. What was he supposed to make of it?

Don't trust her. She already hurt you once.

The little voice in his head continued to issue warnings. But his heart longed to hear her out. There was something more here—something he was missing.

But could he afford to take another chance on her?

Before either of them could say a word, his phone buzzed. He retrieved it from his pocket and stared at the screen. It was the king—a man who didn't go near a phone unless it was urgent.

Demetrius wanted to ignore it. He wanted to finish this conversation, but his royal duties trumped his personal life—just like he'd seen the king do time and again.

He took the call. All it amounted to was a few short, clipped sentences. There was an emergency at the shipping port. A car had been dispatched to pick him up.

When the call was concluded, he turned back to Zoe. "I have to attend to this."

Her face was completely washed out as she nodded but said nothing.

"We aren't finished with this. I'll be back." He strode for the front door.

He wanted to believe that her surprised expression was legitimate. In fact, he'd never wanted anything more in his life, but he couldn't risk it. He couldn't let himself become vulnerable again. Every time he let himself get close to someone—really close—they faded out of his life. First, his mother. Then his wife. And the last blow had been his twin who was now an ocean away with his beautiful bride—not that he could blame him.

But the truth of the matter was Demetrius had given Zoe a chance—he'd given her everything. And in the end, she'd rejected him. How was he supposed to trust her again?

* * *

That can't be right.

We're still married?

Zoe leaned against the back of the couch. Her knees had turned to gelatin.

Thankfully Demetrius had been called away. She needed time to make sense of what he'd said. They were still married? How was that possible?

Once her legs felt a bit steadier, she retrieved her suitcase and moved back through the hallway just off the kitchen. She entered the first spacious bedroom. It was decorated with sunny yellows and perky pinks. The exact opposite of her mood right now.

Demetrius had to be wrong. She was certain she'd signed the papers. She didn't understand. Papers didn't just disappear. What had happened to them?

It was obvious Demetrius wasn't any happier about this development than she was. And now more than ever she needed to make peace with him. He not only held her future in the palm of his hand but also that of her mother. A contract to work on the rest of the revitalization project would make a huge difference in the type of care that Zoe could provide for her mother.

Speaking of her mother, she needed to check in with her. Zoe grabbed her phone and pulled up the number of their friend she was staying with, Liliana. The woman had been their neighbor most of Zoe's childhood. Liliana hadn't just been a friend, she and her husband had quickly become family. Watching Zoe when needed. Sharing holiday meals. And being there for any emergencies.

After a quick greeting, Zoe dove into the reason for her call. "Liliana, how's my mum doing?"

"She has her good days and her bad days. I'm sure you know how that goes."

"I do." It was heartbreaking to watch the confusion that would come over her mother's face—the utter lack of recognition. But thankfully for now the good times outweighed the bad. "I just wanted to let you know that work has me away on a short trip. So you won't reach me at the apartment, but you can always reach me on my cell phone."

"I'm glad to hear that you're getting out and about. You need to do that more often. Too bad the trip is business. Maybe you can squeeze in some fun time."

Demetrius's face flashed in her mind. "I don't think that will be possible. There's a lot of work to do."

"Does this have something to do with that South Shore project?"

"*Sì.*" Zoe knew she had to handle this carefully. Liliana was an astute woman. If Zoe wasn't careful, her friend would add two and two. And there was no doubt about it, Liliana would get four. "I'm doing some research. It appears this project is bigger than I was anticipating."

"Really? That's a good thing, right?"

"It's very good. I just need to be on top of my game."

"Well, don't you worry. Your mother is fine here. She can stay as long as you need."

"Thanks so much. I really appreciate this. Did…did Mum tell you she's moving into assisted living as soon as the arrangements can be made? The doctor suggested that sooner was better than later." The thought that things had deteriorated to that point made Zoe's heart ache.

"I'm so sorry, Zoe. You know I'm just a phone call away."

"*Grazie.*" Liliana was like a second mother to her. "It means a lot."

"This is one of your mother's good days. Would you like to talk with her?"

"I would." Zoe missed her mother dearly. It'd always been the two of them against the world. But lately their roles had started to be reversed and the strong woman that Zoe had always known her mother to be was becoming less and less sure of herself. *Damn disease.*

After a brief talk with her mother, Zoe stowed her unpacked suitcase in the walk-in closet. Not sure whether she was coming or going, she'd deal with it later. Right now, the fresh air beckoned to her. Hopefully a walk on the beach would give her the peace needed to make sense of Demetrius's claim. *They were still married. Husband and wife.* She stared down at her bare ring finger. There had to be an explanation, but what?

Zoe moved to the deck. A long set of wooden steps led her down to the pristine beach. It was so hard to believe that this was all private property—property of the Crown. And she had it all to herself.

The thought brought her no joy. All she could picture was the accusing stare that Demetrius had leveled at her. Why would he think she had something to do with the missing papers when she was the one to end their marriage?

CHAPTER SEVEN

"Zoe, where are you?"

Demetrius stood in the living room of the beach house and raked his fingers through his hair. It'd taken him longer at the palace than he had anticipated. With his twin brother, Alex, in the States with his wife's family, the responsibility for Mirraccino's shipping port fell to Demetrius.

He'd hoped Zoe would have made herself at home, but there was no sign of her. "Zoe!"

Again there was no answer.

Where was she? His mind spun back in time. This wasn't the first time that he'd searched for her, only to find her gone. The last time he'd found a brief note and tracked her down in the palace driveway—where she'd told him that she was leaving. If he hadn't gone after her, she would have left without saying one single word to him. Is that what she'd done again? Had she left?

He rushed back the hallway, checking each bedroom for any sign of her. Each room was empty and there was no sign of her suitcase. His gut churned. Why did he think this time would be any different?

He strode to the deck where he rested his palms on the railing and leaned forward. His gaze stretched out over the crystal-blue water. Gentle swells rose and fell. Usually he could find solace in the water, but not today. All he could think about was how once again she'd skipped out on him. This time there wasn't so much as a note.

His palm smacked the top of the railing. This was it. He was done trying to play nice with her. If she didn't want to deal with him, she could hash it out with the palace's team of attorneys.

Just then a movement on the beach caught his attention. He turned and focused in on the person strolling up the beach. But how was that possible? This beach was protected as part of the royal estate. As the figure drew closer, he quickly recognized the dark ponytail and the purple jacket.

It was Zoe. He stood up straight. She hadn't left after all. He suddenly felt foolish for jumping to conclusions.

She glanced up at him and waved, but she didn't smile. He raised his hand and waved back. He told himself that she didn't still get to him. This whole arrangement was just a means to an end. That was all.

"I thought you'd left," he said as she joined him on the deck. His voice came out gruffer than he'd intended.

Her eyes widened. "Is that your way of telling me to leave?"

"No." He rubbed the back of his neck. "That isn't what I meant."

"Did you get your problem resolved?"

He nodded. "It's dealt with for the moment. Now it's time to deal with our problem."

"You make it sound like your life is a series of problems." She leaned back against the deck rail. "Since when did you get so serious? Weren't you the one that said life is for enjoying?"

He sighed. "That was a long time ago."

"Not that long ago."

A frown pulled at his lips. "I'm fine just the way I am."

"You aren't the same happy guy I used to know."

"I'm happy." Wasn't he? In all honesty, he'd been so focused on living up to people's expectations that he'd dismissed what was important to him.

"But you rarely laugh or smile. It's like you're afraid

your face will crack if you let your guard down and enjoy yourself."

He shook his head, refusing to hear what she was saying. "I enjoy myself...when there's time. I have a lot of things that need my attention. And right now I don't have time to be irresponsible."

"So you decided to take your royal responsibilities seriously?"

"I did. It was time." His work was a refuge from the pain of yet another person he loved disappearing from his life. When Zoe had walked out on him, it'd nearly crushed him.

After his mother's death and the disintegration of his family, Demetrius thought he'd finally found what he'd been searching for when he met Zoe. Warmth, happiness and most of all, love. Life couldn't get any better—or so he'd thought. If only she'd have stayed, he would have moved heaven and earth to make her happy.

"What are you thinking about?" Zoe studied him.

He turned and gazed out over the blue sea. "Us."

There was a noticeable moment of silence. "What about us?"

He wasn't about to admit that he was thinking about their failed marriage. About how his world had crumbled after she'd left. Nor would he admit to how he had to rebuild himself in the aftermath. She didn't deserve to know the damage she'd caused.

He faced her. "I want to know why you walked out on me and yet you refuse to sign the annulment papers." His gaze narrowed in on her. "What's your agenda?"

All of the pain came rushing back to him. He wasn't about to let her plead innocence. He wasn't going to let her run away again—not until he got the answers that had been alluding him this past year.

"Are you holding out for more money?"

"No! How could you think that?"

He left her question unanswered. He had his own questions and they took priority right now. "Are you sure you aren't holding out for a moment in the spotlight? A chance to sell your story to the highest bidder?"

"No. No. No." Hurt reflected in her eyes. "Would you quit with the accusations. I never wanted your money. I wanted—" She pressed her lips together.

At last they were getting somewhere, and he wasn't going to let it drop now. "You wanted what?"

Silence was his only answer.

He stepped forward. She lowered her gaze. Maybe her reason for not signing the papers was something he hadn't considered—not until now. Did she have regrets? Was she hoping for a reconciliation? If so, she was going to have a very long wait.

As though she could read the direction of his thoughts, her head rose. Their gazes caught and held. An old spark of attraction flared to life. This shouldn't happen. He was over her. But the longer she stared into his eyes, the harder it became to remember why this was a bad idea—a very bad idea.

He reached out to her. His fingers traced her cheek. Her skin was soft and subtle. "Is this what you wanted?"

"No." But her voice lacked conviction.

"I think it is. Remember how good we used to be together?"

Her gaze never left his as his fingers trailed down her jaw to trace her lips. Her eyes dilated as she inhaled a swift breath. The little voice in his mind that said he shouldn't be doing this became more and more distant—like the night he insisted they elope. He'd ignored that little voice then and he ignored it now. He had to prove to her that she'd made the biggest mistake of her life when she'd walked away from him. This time he'd be the one doing the walking.

His free hand wrapped around her waist, pulling her voluptuous curves snug against him. Her soft jasmine scent teased his senses. Every time he detected that scent, he thought of her—of her body next to his. It had been so long—so terribly long since he'd been this close to her. She wanted him, too. The passion was there in her eyes.

Buried emotions, desires and longings bubbled to the surface. He needed her—wanted her. The breath hitched in his throat. His head dipped, replacing his fingers with his lips. Her mouth didn't move at first. His touch was gentle, holding back the powerful rush of desire raging through his veins. His heart hammered against his chest.

His mouth brushed over her petal-soft lips. Just as sweet and tempting as he remembered. He wouldn't scare her away—not again. She just needed a moment to remember how amazing they'd been together. No one could forget that—not even him.

The next thing he knew her hands slipped up over his chest and wrapped around the back of his head. Her nails scraped up over his scalp as she pulled him closer. A moan swelled in the back of her throat as their kiss intensified.

He knew it. She still wanted him. If there was one thing they always had going for them, it was chemistry. The distance they'd endured had done one very obvious thing—it'd intensified the sparks arching between them, making them combustible.

Her lips moved with frantic need under his. Her excitement only aroused him more. Somewhere along the way the kiss became less about teaching her a lesson and more about him filling that empty spot in his chest. How had he lived so long without her? Her kisses were like a wellspring of life. They sealed the hollow spots in his scarred heart.

Not about to let this moment end, he scooped her up in his arms. Her hands braced on his chest. She pulled back. Her eyes were filled with a mixture of rousing desire and confusion.

"I thought you might want to continue this inside." His voice came out deeper than normal.

"*Sì*...um, no." She struggled against his hold on her. "Put me down."

"But, Zoe—"

"I mean it. Put me down."

With great regret, he did as she asked and lowered her feet to the ground. His jaw tensed. His back teeth ground together.

The moment had slipped through his fingers just like the whirlwind marriage had slipped past him. One minute they were whispering sweet nothings to each other in their palace suite—the next he was returning from a meeting with the king to find their rooms empty except for a note on his pillow that said, "Sorry. This was a mistake." A blasted note! That was all she had felt it necessary to leave him.

"That shouldn't have happened." Her fingers pressed to her lips.

His gaze challenged her. "You certainly seemed to be enjoying it."

This time she didn't turn away. "I did, but it wasn't right. We can't recapture the past."

How was he supposed to argue when she was the only one making sense right now? He was the one who was supposed to be saying these things. All it'd taken was one kiss and everything had become mixed up and turned around.

He raked his fingers through his hair. They needed to finish this here and now. This time he wouldn't let himself get distracted, no matter how sweet her kisses may be.

"You're right. We can't go back in time." He mentally kicked himself for trying such a stupid stunt. "But that doesn't mean you don't owe me an explanation for running out on me—on our marriage."

"It's too late to get into all of that."

"No, it isn't."

"Fine. If you want to know the truth, it's simple. I left because I'm not right for you. I never was and I never will be."

Frustration churned in his gut. "That isn't an explanation. That's an excuse."

"Trust me. It's all you need to know."

Her unwillingness to be forthcoming only irritated him more.

"Fine. Keep it a secret. You seem to be good at holding things back. It really doesn't matter anymore. But you will explain why you didn't sign and return the annulment papers. So if you don't want money and you obviously aren't interested in a reconciliation, why else continue our marriage?"

CHAPTER EIGHT

He was right about one thing.

Zoe had been holding back but not for the reasons Demetrius was suggesting.

She never imagined how it might look to him. At the time, she'd been so caught up in her fear for her mother's safety to think clearly. A call from the *polizia* had burst the illusion of happily-ever-after. That long-ago call had made her face reality—accept the graveness of her mother's illness.

Until the *polizia* had found her mother wandering the streets in her nightgown, lost and confused, Zoe had been living in a state of denial—unable to accept the harsh sentence this disease was exacting on her mother. It had been all too easy to get caught up in the rush of love—of the promise of a fairy-tale ending—rather than to acknowledge that she was on the verge of losing the one person who meant the world to her. But Zoe didn't have that excuse now—not when Demetrius thought the absolute worst of her.

Her gaze moved to the steps. An escape was so close and yet so far away. The sandy beach looked so inviting. But she couldn't. Not yet. Not until she got to the bottom of this mess.

She rolled back the memories. Though it had all taken place less than a year ago, in so many ways it seemed like a lifetime ago. She clearly remembered the day the annulment papers had arrived. They'd been messengered to her apartment. They'd nearly destroyed her to read, but somehow she found the strength to pen her name on them. As for the check, she just couldn't accept the money, especially after the way things had ended. She clearly recalled ripping it into itty-bitty pieces.

At the time, things had been so hectic. Her mother's situation had been in flux. There were doctors' appointments. And with her mother's rapidly declining condition, lots of tests. But Zoe was certain she'd taken care of the annulment papers.

Her head started to pound. "I know I signed the papers. I...I don't know what happened to them after that. A clerk must have misplaced them because I don't have them."

"And that's it? That's your only explanation?"

"*Si!* Do you really find that so hard to believe?"

He paused as though really giving some thought to the possibility there could have been a clerical snafu. "I'll check into it."

"Your words say one thing but your eyes say another." She frowned at him. "Why do you find it so hard to believe that I'm not behind the missing papers?"

"Because it wouldn't be the first time you lied to me."

She pressed her hands to her hips and lifted her chin. "What's that supposed to mean?"

"It means you lied when you married me. You said you loved me, yet when our marriage hit a few snags, you cut and ran—"

"That's not true. I had to. I..." Realizing that he was in absolutely no frame of mind to comprehend what she was about to say, she pressed her lips together and turned away.

"You didn't have to run away. I told you numerous times that we'd work it out with the king and his counsel. We'd have found a way to sway the public's support."

"I know you tried. And...and I wanted to believe you. I desperately wanted to believe that everything would fall into place. But it didn't. Don't you understand, my leaving was for the best?"

"The best for whom? Me? Not hardly. You knew that I loved you. So it must have been best for you. Did leaving make you happy?"

She didn't say anything. She really did owe him an explanation but not now—not with him tossing around blame. He was justifiably angry. She knew all too well about anger. She'd spent the past year angry at the entire world. In the end, the anger had been easier for her to deal with than the acceptance of what was happening to her mother and the fact that Demetrius would be better off without her.

"Well?" he persisted.

"No. It didn't make me happy. But I did what I had to do. I didn't have a choice."

Demetrius's dark brows rose. "Wait. Are you saying that the king forced you out?"

Her temples throbbed. "I…I…"

"What? I need to know. You owe me that much."

"Not now. I can't do this." Her feet barely brushed over the steps as she made her escape from the disappointment and hurt reflected in Demetrius's eyes. She knew that she'd put it there, and she couldn't stand it. And it didn't matter what she said now, it wouldn't fix it.

Sometimes it didn't matter how much power or money a person had, they couldn't fix everything. There was no reversing her mother's condition and there was no way to change the fact that most likely her own DNA was corrupted with the devious disease that would slowly steal away a lifetime of memories and worse.

"Zoe! Wait!" Demetrius's agitated voice called out to her. "Zoe, don't run away again!"

She couldn't stop. Her knees pumped up and down. Harder. Faster. Her bare feet moved over the now-cold sand. She had no destination in mind. No finish line. She just had to keep going—putting distance between herself and Demetrius.

But it didn't matter how far she went, his words followed her. They dug inside her, poking at all of her tender spots. Was he right?

Was she running away?

She stopped. Her heart pounded. She drew one deep breath after another into her straining lungs. And still Demetrius's words were all she could hear over and over in her mind.

Don't run away again.

She'd never thought about it before. She'd never stopped to even consider her actions. She dropped to her knees, covering her face with her hands. He couldn't be right. Could he? Was that what she did? Run away?

Her mind started to replay the events since she'd met him. First her mother's diagnosis—the diagnosis that Zoe refused to accept. And what had she done, she'd run into Demetrius's arms.

And just after the royal counsel pointed out that she wouldn't live up to the king's expectations for a princess, there was the urgent phone call from the *polizia*. They'd found her mother wandering the streets—proof that she really wasn't fit to be princess. Not wanting Demetrius to pity her—to stay with her out of obligation—she'd run.

Later, she'd told herself that it was the shock and the fear for her mother that had her dashing off a note to Demetrius before she disappeared into the night. But the truth was that it was easier to run than to stand her ground—to face the pain she'd caused him.

Why hadn't she seen this before? Why did Demetrius see her biggest weakness so clearly when she'd been blind to it? It seemed she was more like her absentee father than she'd ever imagined.

Because of her mother, Zoe had finally stopped running. Zoe was doing her best to be steady for her ailing mother. Now it was time that she stood still and faced the problems with Demetrius—her husband. After all, if her mother could face Alzheimer's with dignity, Zoe could deal with her broken heart.

She got to her feet.

It was time she spoke openly and honestly with her husband.

When she made it back to the beach house, it was dark. "Demetrius." She turned on the lights in the living room. No sign of him. "Demetrius, are you here?"

No answer.

He'd left. Disappointment assailed her. She couldn't be upset with him. It was no less than she'd done to him. Twice now.

In and out of meetings all of the next day, Demetrius finally arrived at the palace offices to find Zoe gathering her things together. He glanced at his watch. "I guess it is time to call it quits for the day."

She glanced up as though she wasn't aware he'd entered the room. "I'll be out of the office most of tomorrow. In fact, probably all of it. I need to go to the mansion for photos and measurements. And then I need to do some shopping—"

He held up his hand, stopping her gush of words. "It's okay. You don't have to tell me your every move. And please feel free to use the car I've put at your disposal."

Surprise flashed in her eyes. "*Grazie*." She zipped her computer case and headed for the door. As though it were an afterthought, she turned back. "Good night."

"Zoe. Wait." She hesitated in the doorway, eventually turning around to face him. He wasn't sure how to say this, but he'd give it his best try. "About last night. I handled it poorly. I guess I'm not as over it as I thought."

Her eyes grew shiny and she blinked repeatedly. "I'm so sorry for everything."

After Zoe had hedged around the fact that his father

might have had something to do with her leaving, he just wouldn't—couldn't—leave it alone. Unable to harness his emotions, he'd gone to his father and laid out the stark facts. His father, confronted with these allegations, had aged right before Demetrius's eyes. The king admitted that he hadn't handled the news of the elopement as well as he should have, but he swore on all that was precious to him that he hadn't run off Zoe.

Before Demetrius could tell Zoe what had happened, she turned and disappeared down the hallway. Part of him said to let her go, but another part of him knew that this thing between them had to be resolved. They couldn't continue to work together in this emotionally charged atmosphere.

She'd told him what she knew about the annulment papers, now he needed to stop pushing her for an answer about what happened to their marriage. It hadn't been his father. It hadn't been anything but the fact that she hadn't loved him enough to take on this intimidating life of royalty. And he had to stop blaming her for that—for refusing to live a lie.

He dropped his tablet on the desk and headed down the hallway. The only problem was the palace was a maze of hallways. Zoe could have gone in any direction.

"Are you looking for Zoe?" Annabelle stopped next to him.

At that particular moment, he didn't care what rumors he might start, he had to find her. "Did you see which way she went?"

Annabella pointed toward the front staircase. "She was in a hurry. I don't know if you'll catch her."

He took long, quick strides until he was in the driveway. The car he'd put at her disposal was still parked. Well, that was a good sign. He still had a chance of finding her.

The young driver came rushing over. "Sir, may I help you?"

"Did you see Ms. Sarris?"

He nodded. "She said that she wouldn't need a ride this evening, sir. She said she wanted to walk."

"Which way did she go?"

The young man pointed toward the beach.

Demetrius set off after her. Still in a suit and tie, he wasn't exactly dressed for a stroll on the beach, but that didn't stop him. He was intent on setting things straight. He told himself that it was purely a business decision. The strain between them wasn't conducive to productivity.

He set off down the long set of steps at the back of the palace. They stretched down the cliff to the pristine beach below. He paused midway down the stairs and searched the shoreline. He immediately spotted her standing at the edge of the water, staring off into the distant horizon where the setting sun hovered low in the azure sky.

As he rushed down the remaining stairs, he wondered what was going through her mind. At one point he'd been able to read her thoughts or so he liked to think. Back when they were together there had been times when a deep sadness was reflected in her eyes. It seemingly came from nowhere and when he asked her about it, she brushed it off and changed the subject. He never wanted to be responsible for causing her such pain, but last night he'd done just that and he'd witnessed that same look of pain again—pain he'd inflicted.

He stopped behind her. "Zoe."

She didn't move, but he knew that she'd heard him. Maybe it'd be easier this way. "I wanted to apologize. I was out of line last night. I'm not going to make excuses. I just want you to know that it won't happen again." Still, she didn't move. He deserved her cold shoulder. "You should know that I confronted the king. He feels bad about not being more welcoming. I also initiated an investigation into the missing annulment papers."

Zoe spun around.

"Why would you do that? Does Annabelle know?"

Why did she keep worrying about Annabelle? Had they become that good of friends so quickly? Was she worried that Annabelle would stop talking to her if she knew they were married? He had to admit that he didn't know much about the ways of women's minds, but Annabelle didn't strike him as the petty type.

"You don't have to worry. Even if Annabelle knew the truth about us, she'd still be your friend."

Zoe shook her head. "I don't think so. Although I'm surprised you haven't confided in her. Don't you think she should know?"

"No, I don't." He and Annabelle were acquaintances at best.

"If I was planning to marry you, I'd want to know that you already have a wife—"

"Marry?" What? Had he heard her correctly? "Annabelle and I?"

Zoe nodded. "She's perfect for you. An aristocrat's daughter. Your country will have a strong ally in Halencia."

"Stop!" The unintentional boom of his voice had Zoe's eyes opening wide. He made a point of lowering his voice. "Annabelle and I are not getting married."

"But after the annulment is resolved—"

"Not then. Not ever."

Zoe's brow wrinkled. "I don't understand."

"Neither do I. Annabelle isn't in Mirraccino to get married. Her father didn't approve of her globe-trotting, partying ways. He thought a job would teach her some responsibility. Her father and my father put their heads together. In exchange for Annabelle being the face of the South Shore revitalization project that includes advertisements and billboards, her father agreed to be a large investor in the project. He will be attending the Royal Christmas Ball."

"He's one of the people you need to impress?"

Demetrius nodded. "Now do you understand? Annabelle has nothing to do with you and me."

"But you can't launch a search for the annulment papers. People will talk. Rumors will start. What if the media finds out about you and me?"

He rubbed the back of his neck. The muscles were tense and giving him a headache. "Honestly, I'm surprised the paparazzi hasn't found out by now."

"But you've worked so hard to change your public persona—to get the people to respect you—"

"And I have no intention of smearing my name. Everything will be done hush-hush under the direction of counsel." He was struck by her genuine concern. If there was any doubt whatsoever of whether she'd signed the annulment papers or not, he had his answer now.

"I hope they find them before someone else does."

"I do, too. But we'll deal with that issue if we have to."

"So you believe me? You believe I wasn't going to use the papers against you?"

He shifted his weight from foot to foot. "I still have questions, but no, I don't think you were planning to blackmail me or anything."

"I guess that will have to be enough."

He wasn't sure where that left them, but he'd take it as a good sign. After all, there was no reason they had to be enemies. There were plenty of exes who were friends. Weren't there?

"It's a nice evening for a walk. How about I walk you back to the beach house?"

Surprise lit up her eyes. He thought for sure that she'd turn him down. He still wasn't so sure he could pull off this friend thing, not when he remembered vividly the sweetness of her kisses. But he wanted to give it a try. They'd done the fighting thing and it wasn't working for him. It was time for a change.

Zoe nodded. "I'd like that."

"So would I."

Side by side, they strolled down the beach as the sun sunk lower on the horizon and the water rolled farther up the beach. When a strong breeze rushed past them, Zoe rubbed her arms and he realized she wasn't wearing a jacket. He slipped off his suit coat and placed it over her shoulders.

After all, that's what friends do—look out for each other. With a little practice, he just might be able to pull this friendship off. And it felt so much better than arguing.

CHAPTER NINE

A PEACEFUL COEXISTENCE had formed.

Dare she call it a friendship?

Zoe had her hands full traveling between Residenza del Rosa, the palace and the beach house. Days turned into a week and then two weeks as rush orders were placed for state-of-the-art office furniture. The pieces were needed for the administrative suite on the second floor of the mansion. Those offices needed to be smart looking as well as functional. That was the easy part.

The common rooms on the first floor would take more effort—more creativity. They would have a different function and hopefully portray a more relaxed mood.

Today, the painting should be underway. She was anxious to see if the shades they'd settled on were the same calming colors once it covered the entire wall. She crossed her fingers for luck. They were running out of time to have additional colors specially mixed and delivered.

The royal sedan pulled right up to the front of the mansion. She immediately noticed that the construction equipment had been removed. New sod had been laid on the front lawn. The end was in sight. When she stepped out of the vehicle, she could still hear some smaller machines as they worked on the back of the building. If she had to guess, she'd say they were working on the landscaping.

Suddenly she got the feeling she was being watched. The hairs on the back of her neck lifted. She looked around as she started up the steps to Residenza del Rosa.

This time, there weren't any reporters or photographers waiting, but there was something different—the royal security detail was out and about. She was quite certain they weren't there to secure her safety.

Demetrius was there. Somewhere. Her stomach fluttered with nerves.

She reached the landing at the same moment he stepped out of the front door. He stood there in the early morning sunshine looking quite regal in his navy suit. The top buttons of his shirt were undone giving the slightest hint of his tanned, muscular chest. She knew that chest inch by inch, and she recalled how he had this one ticklish spot on his right side—

She jerked her meandering thoughts to a sudden halt. She couldn't go there. No way. Not even now that she knew they were legally husband and wife. She didn't want to jeopardize this brand-new friendship.

Demetrius strode over to her. "Are you that disappointed at seeing me?"

"What? Um. No. Just surprised is all."

"Well, if you keep frowning like that when we're together, rumors are going to start."

"Oh." She immediately smiled.

"That's much better."

He was so handsome. Her gaze moved from his strong jaw, to his kissable lips and up to his eyes that were staring back at her. Her heart tip-tapped. *Remember to keep things light. Don't ruin things.*

She swallowed hard. "What's brought you here this morning?"

"I was just notified that all of the invitations for the Royal Christmas Ball have gone out to the select group of guests. I need to make sure that everything here is progressing as planned. Are there any problems I should be aware of?"

Again, she had the feeling she was being watched. She glanced around. Who was it? She grew frustrated, not being able to locate anyone. Maybe she was just being paranoid after her run-ins with that persistent reporter.

"Zoe, did you hear me?"

"Um, what?" She didn't want to mention anything and sound paranoid. After all, it was just a feeling. Thankfully, she hadn't seen the creepy reporter in a few weeks, not since the night Demetrius showed up at her apartment. Surely by now he'd given up.

Demetrius's brows drew together. "Zoe, what's the matter? You haven't heard a word I've said."

She gave the area one last glance before turning her full attention back to Demetrius. "The progress of the mansion is on schedule. As of right now, the administrative suite upstairs is painted and scheduled to be carpeted tomorrow. The furniture is being shipped express. The staff will be able to move in shortly. I know that's a priority." She started for the entrance. "As for the common rooms, I've been in daily contact with the various contractors. In fact, today the paint is already going up on the walls."

Demetrius stopped just outside the front door and turned to her. "Listen, I've been meaning to tell you that you've done a really good job with this project so far."

"Really?" His compliment made her heart do the tip-tap-tap rhythm again. "But you haven't even seen it yet."

"I've seen the progression of your sketches and I know that you've been on top of the whole project. I'm certain that it's going to turn heads."

"*Grazie*. And I don't just mean for your kind words. I mean for giving me this great opportunity."

"It wasn't altruistic. I needed the best, and you are it. A rising star."

It felt so strange to talk to him like this, but she eagerly welcomed the friendly words. "Shall we go inside and see how the color scheme is panning out?"

He nodded. He pulled the door open for her.

She stepped inside the foyer and was immediately greeted by the serenity of blue walls with a cloud-white trim. It all blended beautifully with the white marble floor woven with a gray-and-brown mineral pattern. She smiled. So far so good.

A gentle breeze rushed past her carrying with it the scent of fresh paint. She loved the smell. It meant that one of her many sketches was being brought to life. Her hands clenched as a mixture of excitement and worry collided. There were times when projects didn't turn out quite as expected. *Please don't let this be one of those times.*

She couldn't wait to see the ballroom. It was to be the shimmering jewel of this entire project. She turned in that direction when she heard Demetrius clear his throat.

She stifled a sigh and turned. "Did you have someplace in particular that you wanted to start?"

He nodded in the opposite direction. "I thought we'd take a look at the garden. I know you weren't in charge of it, but your vision for the interior greatly influenced the approach they took."

She had to admit that she was anxious to see the garden. Her mother had a fondness for them. In fact, Zoe thought her mother would approve of Residenza del Rosa. Now, if only Zoe could figure out how to get her mother a room in the exclusive and expensive center. She had a feeling a deep and honest conversation was on the horizon between her and the administrator of the facility. She wasn't above begging if that's what it took.

She followed Demetrius down the hallway to a doorway that led to the courtyard surrounded in the distance by a low wall. They stepped out onto the freshly laid mosaic tiles. They were of earthy red tones offset by a bright blue-and-white pattern.

The walkway led to a center patio with an old fountain that had been lovingly restored. The tiles there contained seashell outlines. Someone had the foresight to continue the theme by surrounding the edge of the patio with crushed shells.

Demetrius pointed to the edge of the patio. "There will be benches added so people can come out here to enjoy a bit of the day or to entertain company."

"I love it." Her gaze met his. Her heart picked up its pace. "They're doing a fabulous job."

"I'm so glad you approve. I told the gardener that the courtyard would have to be extra special so it didn't detract from the interior design."

Heat warmed her cheeks over his compliment. She turned away, glancing around as a few men were hard at work digging spots for a variety of plants, from olive trees to medium palms and citrus trees. There was other foliage that Zoe couldn't name. But she liked it…a lot.

Zoe's gaze lingered over the potted plants with brilliant red, lemon yellow and spicy-orange blooms. All were waiting to be transplanted into the rich soil. She could already envision the garden completely finished. It would be wonderful. She would definitely spend some time here if given the opportunity. She hoped the residents would find it just as appealing.

Demetrius turned to her. "I take it you approve of the decision to refurbish the fountain."

She nodded. "You can't find that sort of detail these days. And the fish and seashell design will go splendidly with what I'm doing with the inside."

"I thought you might approve. There's still quite a bit of work they need to do out here, but it should be completed in time for the big reveal."

"Good." She glanced up. His gaze met hers causing her heart to thump rapidly.

Ever since she'd learned that he was still her husband, it was as if she was seeing him differently. He was no longer the impulsive guy that she'd initially fallen for. There was so much more to Demetrius than she'd noticed before. And she found herself falling for him all over again.

He had quite a brilliant head for business. He was a natural at taking control of not only his emotions but also emotional situations. He thought before he acted. This was a man she felt confident would one day be a good leader for their nation.

He was also good for her—whether she wanted to admit it or not. Though he could make her heart race like no other, he could also put her at ease as though nothing in this world was insurmountable, which was ridiculous considering her mother's irreversible diagnosis. But somehow, he still made her want to believe in dreams and the power of love.

She knew she was setting herself up for a fall. Sooner, rather than later, this unconventional marriage would end—for real this time.

She dreaded that quickly approaching day.

Demetrius escorted Zoe around Residenza del Rosa, paying her more attention than the restoration work being done on the historic mansion. But he couldn't help it. Zoe kept sending him strange looks. He wanted to stop her and ask what was on her mind. Was she thinking about the fact they were still secretly married?

He couldn't tell if that knowledge came to her as good news or bad news. Not that he cared. Well, maybe he was just a bit curious. Okay, a lot curious.

After inspecting the shell pink paint in the sunroom and the sandy shades in the library, they made their way back to the reception area. He'd asked the foreman to gather the workmen together. He wanted to give them a word of encouragement.

While waiting for everyone to be assembled, a few of the men approached him to discuss the revitalization project.

The men were friendly and thankful for the work. Demetrius promised to do all he could to keep the revitalization project alive.

When it came time for the talk, Demetrius motioned for Zoe to join him. She stepped forward. As strange as it sounded, it felt natural having her next to him. Dare he admit it, he liked having her back in his life.

He cleared his throat. "Ms. Sarris and I would like to thank you all for doing such wonderful work. This place looks amazing. I know this isn't the sort of place people want to end up, but I'm hoping Ms. Sarris's vision will give the place a fresh and easy air. I know that we don't have much time until the Christmas ball and the official opening in the New Year, but I personally appreciate all of the extra time and effort you've put into this very special project. Give yourselves a round of applause."

Demetrius started clapping. Zoe joined him and then one by one the men started clapping and smiling.

When silence fell back over the room, Demetrius had one more announcement. "I'm so impressed that each of you will be receiving a Christmas bonus if the project is brought in a week early."

Another round of clapping. Cheers and whistles went up.

"Okay, men, let's get back to it," the foreman said.

"Kiss. Kiss. Kiss." A soft chant started.

What in the world? Demetrius's first thought was to glance at Zoe to see if she had any clue what they were talking about, but he didn't dare look in her direction. He didn't want anyone to read anything in his expression.

"Kiss. Kiss." The chant grew louder and some started to clap. There were smiles all around.

Demetrius turned a questioning look to the foreman. The man pointed upward. Demetrius tilted his head back, already suspecting what he'd find. Mistletoe.

Something told him that the workers had a bit of holiday

mischief going on as he recalled how they'd pointed out where he should stand to give this talk. He tried to figure out which man had suggested this particular spot. Demetrius was unable to locate him in the crowd.

And still the chanting continued.

Not seeing an easy way out of this awkward spot, he turned to Zoe to see if she'd been wise enough to make a hasty exist. This time he wouldn't blame her for running away. But much to his surprise she was still standing there frozen. Worry, or was it panic, reflected in her eyes. A kiss certainly wasn't going to help his resolve to keep their relationship on friendly terms.

Still, he didn't know how to just walk away without turning this awkward situation into a big deal. He glanced out at the sea of smiling faces. Their jolly moods were good for business. And if he walked out now, he knew there would be a distinct shift in attitude. Too bad he'd thrown out the Christmas bonuses before this mistletoe scene. He'd lost a very effective distraction.

"Kiss. Kiss. Kiss."

This wasn't a good idea. And yet...

"Kiss."

This was a really bad idea. But still...

"Kiss."

Demetrius leaned toward her and her eyes opened wide, but it was her glossy lips that beckoned to him. He wanted—no—he needed to once again feel her lips beneath his. He longed to taste her sweet kiss again. In fact, he'd never wanted something so much in his life.

But at the last second, he moved, letting his lips land on her cheek. It definitely wasn't what he'd had in mind, but it was for the best. The crowd went crazy. Applause made any attempt at conversation nearly impossible.

The quick and simple kiss was over in a heartbeat. When Zoe's gaze met his, his heart thumped hard. In fact, it was beating so loud that he was sure she could hear it. How was it that a woman who'd hurt him so deeply could have such a tremendous effect on him?

Perhaps he'd been working too much—for far too many hours. That had to be it. Because he was over Zoe. He'd put her in his rearview mirror that dark, overcast night when she'd left without an explanation. They were friends now. Nothing more.

He turned away from her. It was then that he noticed a number of phones pointed in their direction. So their little bit of fun had been photographed. That was a complication he hadn't anticipated. It seemed that when Zoe was around, there were quite a few things that slipped his mind.

But he didn't have to worry. His security team was all over it. Demetrius breathed an easy breath as phones were confiscated and photos of himself and Zoe were deleted. Apparently the men had forgotten that upon being hired for this very special project—a project that he planned to oversee personally—that they'd signed confidentiality agreements.

The part of this whole scenario that alarmed Demetrius was that after everything, Zoe still got to him. He'd have to be careful in the future. Keep more of a distance in their friendship.

He wouldn't give her a chance to hurt him again.

CHAPTER TEN

TIME TO MAKE a hasty exit.

Zoe didn't even wait for Demetrius as she moved away—far away from the mistletoe. Her heart was still hammering. She'd thought for sure he was going to lay a real kiss on her—in front of everyone. And the truth was, she wouldn't have stopped him. Did that make her desperate? Or was she just plain pathetic?

She gave a shake of her head as she rushed past the newly erected registration desk toward the grand ballroom. She didn't need any distractions right now—even if it was from the sexiest prince on the planet. She needed to concentrate on her work. Everything had to be perfect for the Royal Christmas Ball. She wouldn't let Demetrius down this time. She owed him that much.

Before she reached the ballroom, she felt a hand on her shoulder. She paused and turned, not quite ready to discuss what had happened back there.

Demetrius stood before her with a frown on his face. "What are you running from?"

"I wasn't running." Was she?

"It sure looked like it to me."

Drat. She wanted to show Demetrius that she was changing. That she wasn't the same person he used to know. She was done running. She was working hard at facing her problems head-on. At least most of them.

"Well, you are mistaken." She wondered how many people had the nerve to say that to the prince. "I was excited is all." Then realizing that her words could be misconstrued, she added, "Excited to see how the ballroom turned out."

His eyes reflected disbelief. "You know, you don't have to worry."

"Who said I was worried?" She forced a smile to her lips.

"No one has to say it. It's written all over your face. The thing you don't know is that all of the people on this job site signed a confidentiality agreement. They can't share any photos of me or talk to the press about what they witness here. In fact, my security team confiscated their phones and deleted the photos."

"Really?"

He nodded. "Do you feel better?"

"*Sì.*" The worry of the paparazzi spinning one innocent holiday kiss out of control slid off her shoulders. "Come on. Let's go see it." She reached for his hand to pull him along with her.

Her fingers slid over his warm palm. Her fingertips curled around his hand and she started toward the ballroom. Then she realized that she couldn't be this familiar with the prince in public. Not unless she really did want people to talk. With much regret, she loosened her grip, but when she tried to withdraw her hand, he held on.

Her pulse quickened and her heart raced. In her imagination, she envisioned turning to him. He'd gaze into her eyes just before his head dipped and he kissed her properly. This time there'd be no anger. Instead, there'd be a sweetness to it—a yearning for two souls to blend as one.

A frustrated sigh passed her lips.

"What's the matter?"

He had heard her? She'd have to do better at concealing her thoughts. "Nothing. Nothing at all." He sent her an I-don't-believe-you look, but before he could say more, she added, "Let's go see the ballroom. When I checked on it yesterday, I thought it was coming along wonderfully."

The oversized, white doors with gold trim were propped open and she rushed past them. The breath caught in her throat as she took in the massive changes to the room. The Roman pillars she'd insisted Demetrius splurge on lined both sides of the room. On the far side, between the pillars, were two sets of French doors. They led to a private terrace.

She turned to find Demetrius standing directly behind her. "What do you think?"

"I think you are very good at your job."

A smile pulled at her lips. *He liked it. He really liked it.*

"And best of all, after the ball is over there is furniture ordered to make this an all-purpose room. Couches will be added on the side with the French doors. A group of tables will be added at the far end for card or board games. And over at the other end will be a bunch of armchairs and end tables for families to get together and visit."

"It seems you've thought of everything."

"I doubt it, but I've really tried to make this place as comfortable for everyone as possible."

"I'm sure they'll appreciate all of your hard work."

"But there's something missing." She stepped into the middle of the room and turned all around. The smile slipped from her lips. She turned around again. This time slower. There was definitely something missing.

"What has you frowning? Is it the pillars, because I have to admit that you were right about them? They are exactly what a room this size needed."

She shook her head. "It's not the pillars. It's something else."

"Maybe it's the paint. I think they only have up the first coat."

"No. That's not it, either." She turned in a circle again. This time her gaze stopped on the interior wall. It was blank. Empty. Boring. "That's it."

"What's it?"

"See this wall." She moved to stand directly in front of it. "It needs something."

"What do you have in mind? A group of paintings?"

She shook her head. "That would be a waste of the space."

"Then what?"

And then it came to her like someone had just switched on a lightbulb. "A mural."

"A what?"

"You heard me. A mural would be perfect here."

He stepped next to her. "Are you sure?"

"Of course I'm sure or I wouldn't have said it." Her mind conjured up all sorts of scenes to fill this blank canvas.

"I guess you do know what you're talking about. But where would we find an artist at the last minute capable of doing such work?"

"I think I know someone who can do it."

"You do?" He turned and looked at her. "Are they available?"

She shrugged and didn't meet his gaze. Maybe she shouldn't have mentioned it. Demetrius would probably find her idea preposterous when she told him the name of the artist.

"Zoe, are you trying to tell me that you want to paint it?"

This was her chance to put her artwork out there—to spread her wings so to speak. Besides, this was about the people who would eventually live here. They needed a welcoming, relaxing atmosphere, and she was convinced a mural would be just the ticket to pull the whole design together. "*Sì.*"

He rubbed his jaw as though seriously considering her proposal. That had to be a good sign, right? She willed him to go with the idea. Her mother for one would love it—if only Zoe could get her a room in the upscale residence.

Unable to take the silence any longer, she uttered, "Well, what do you think?"

* * *

Zoe pleaded with Demetrius with her eyes.

How could he deny her this?

He could feel any reservations he might have folding like a house of cards. "I think it'll be perfect."

She clapped her hands together in excitement. "Great! I can't wait to start."

Demetrius stared up at the big blank wall. A mural certainly would turn heads. But it was a huge task. The interior design already had Zoe so busy. He didn't want her to wear herself out. "Are you sure you're up for an additional project?"

Her face glowed with happiness. "I'm positive. The design is done. The color combinations work. The furniture is ordered. There's nothing pressing at this point that requires my constant attention."

"Okay. You've sold me on the idea."

"You won't be sorry. This is going to be fantastic."

Her enthusiasm was contagious. He'd seen a little of her artwork in the past from her sketch pads. And she'd also shown him pictures of some paintings, mostly landscapes. They were colorful and captivating.

There was still one thing nagging at him—the time element. He stared up at the big blank wall. It was a wide-open space and he couldn't help but wonder how long it'd take to paint a mural. He honestly didn't have any clue.

"What's bothering you?" Zoe's voice drew him out of his thoughts.

"I was wondering how long it'd take to paint a mural."

The light in her eyes dimmed. "You don't think I can do it—"

"That isn't what I said—what I meant. I know that you're very talented and you can do anything you set your mind to. But do you have enough time for such a large project? Do you even know what you'd paint?"

She glanced up at the wall as though giving his words serious consideration. "I know you're hesitant to add something new to the mix at this late stage, but I have a proposition for you."

His ears immediately perked up. So did other parts of him. "What exactly do you have in mind?"

Her eyes widened at the sound of his deep, sultry voice. "Not what you have going on in that dirty mind of yours."

A deep chuckle rumbled in his chest. "Hey, now you're the one throwing around propositions."

She smiled and shook her head. "I'm glad to see there's still some of the Demetrius I used to know lurking about."

She was right. The new Demetrius—the proper one—wouldn't be flirting and playing with innuendos. Maybe he'd taken the role of crown prince too seriously. He rubbed the back of his neck. "About the mural, what are you suggesting?"

"I have some sketches I'd like to show you. They're at my apartment. I have one in particular of the beach that I think would be perfect. But I'll let you pick which sketch I paint."

"Okay. Let's go get them."

"What?" She looked at him as if he'd just spoken in a foreign language.

"We'll pick up your sketch on the way back to the beach house."

She shook her head. "No. Never mind."

He didn't understand the problem. He was willing to entertain her idea and now she was changing her mind. What in the world had he missed?

His gaze met hers. "You no longer want to do the mural?"

"I want to do it."

"Good. But if you think you're going back to your apartment alone with that reporter snooping around then you're mistaken. It's my fault that he's bothering you—"

"No, it isn't."

He arched a brow. "We both know it is. He wants a scoop on the crown prince. The more scandalous, the better. And I'm not going to let him near you."

"You can't always be there to protect me."

She was right and he didn't like it, not one little bit. "But I'm here now."

Her unwavering gaze met his. "Are you sure you have time?"

"I'm sure. Let's go."

CHAPTER ELEVEN

IT WILL ALL work out.

That was what Zoe kept telling herself.

She sat next to Demetrius in the same unmarked black sedan that had escorted her to Residenza del Rosa. Demetrius wanted to stir the least amount of public attention as possible. Although with his security detail in the lead with another black car and an additional black car following closely behind, they stood out even here in the capital of Mirraccino. She tried to reason with him to delay the trip, but he was insistent they move on this immediately.

Frantically, she tried to remember what condition she'd left the apartment in when she'd rushed out the door. Sure he'd been there before, but only for a few minutes, most of which he'd spent standing in the hallway. And then he'd been so concerned about the creepy reporter that she doubted he'd noticed much of anything as he rushed off to speak with his security detail.

Had she put away the dishes? Was there still some lingerie on the drying rack? And that basket of laundry—was it still sitting in the living room? Or had she put the clothes away?

She'd always been able to keep him away from her apartment when they were dating. That hadn't been too hard considering their relationship had been kept on the down low. If her mother had known she was dating the prince, her mother never would have been able to keep the exciting news to herself. Not that Zoe could blame her. At times, she'd felt like she would burst, holding in the fact that she'd found her very own Prince Charming.

"Are you feeling okay?" There was a note of concern in Demetrius's voice.

"Sure. I'm fine. Why wouldn't I be?"

He studied her intently. "You know that you can talk to me about whatever is on your mind?"

Why did things have to be so complicated between them? She longed for a normal life. One where her mother was healthy and could live on her own. One where her mother didn't get confused and frustrated with aspects of life that so many people took for granted.

"Why does life have to be so unfair?" Zoe muttered under her breath.

"Sometimes I wonder the same thing. Being a prince doesn't give me a pass on painful and unhappy moments." Demetrius reached out and wrapped an arm around her shoulders. "I am here if you need me."

At first, she resisted the pull of his arm, but needing to feel his strength and the comfort of someone being on her side, she gave in. Her head came to rest against his shoulder. The scent of his spicy cologne taunted her, reminding her of all the things in life she'd had to give up in order to do right by the people she loved. And now, she had to be content with this platonic touch.

All too soon the car rolled to a stop behind Zoe's apartment building. She reached for the door handle. "Stay here. I'll be right back."

"Not so fast." Demetrius followed her out the door. A bodyguard leaned over and whispered something in Demetrius's ear. "We're clear to go up."

"How do you know?"

He sent her a knowing smile as though he was always two steps ahead of her. "Some of my men were sent ahead to secure the area."

"It must be tough always having to be so careful where

you go and having to be surrounded by your own private army." She truly meant it. She might not be rich, but she did have her privacy and the freedom to come and go as she pleased.

He shrugged. "It is what it is. I'm sorry that it bothers you."

"I…no, it doesn't. It's just so different from my life."

He truly didn't seem fazed by it. Even when he'd been living life to its fullest as the playboy prince when they'd first met, he'd still been surrounded by bodyguards. Demetrius insisted that the men dress to fit in with the crowd. These days, those same bodyguards wore dark suits and dark glasses. There was no missing the fact that they were part of his security detail, and the expression on their faces said that they meant business.

When Zoe stepped into the darkened hallway of the older building, she paused and turned to him. "You really don't have to come with me. I'm sure you have phone calls and other things to do."

His brows rose and for a moment he didn't say anything. "I promise you that you have my undivided attention."

Any other time, she would have loved to be the center of his attention, but not right now. Knowing no other way to deter him from following her to the humble little apartment she shared with her mother, she mounted the steps to the second floor.

All the while, she kept telling herself that it didn't matter. Once this project was done…once the annulment papers were recovered…she'd never see Demetrius again, aside from the photos in the newspaper and the television appearances. Still, she'd have her memories for as long as they lasted. She could only hope they weren't snatched away like her mother's—only to be replaced with confusion and uncertainty.

* * *

Her discomfort was palpable.

Demetrius followed Zoe up the stairs. Her shoulders were rigid. She didn't say a word. He wished she would relax. She didn't have to be self-conscious about the apartment building. Sure it was older and there was nothing fancy about it, but there was an air of hominess—a warmth that at times was lacking from the glamor of the palace now that his mother was no longer around.

Zoe paused outside a brown wooden door. Gold numerals read 213. She turned to him, her gaze not quite reaching his. "My place...it's nothing fancy."

"It's okay, Zoe. Remember, I've been here before." Without thinking of the implications, he reached out and stroked his fingers over her silky smooth cheek. "Stop worrying. It doesn't matter what it looks like. Not everyone is born into a palace. Sometimes, I think you ended up with the better end of the deal."

She sent him a disbelieving look. He couldn't blame her. He realized looking from the outside in that it was hard to believe that life within the palace walls was anything but perfect and worry free.

Sometimes he wondered if part of the problem was that the palace was just so massively big that as a child he sometimes felt as though he got lost amongst the statues and paintings. His mother and father were always hosting an event or entertaining a dignitary. As a kid, he'd promised himself that when he had his own family that he'd always have time for them.

The head of his security detail approached Zoe and requested the key to her apartment. She hesitantly handed it over. With instructions to wait in the hallway with two other bodyguards while the apartment was searched, Zoe crossed her arms and stared at the floor.

"I forget that you aren't used to these security procedures." Feeling as though he owed her a better explanation, he went on. "Lately, there has been a spike in chatter about a revolt. That's why my brother took it upon himself to keep our..." he lowered his voice "...our marriage a secret. He didn't want to give the rebel rousers any help with their cause until the palace figured out how best to present our marriage to the people."

"I didn't know. No one told me."

"No one wanted to worry you." He almost added that he'd warned everyone to keep this from her because he hadn't wanted to scare her off, but it didn't matter. She'd run off anyhow.

The bodyguard reemerged from the apartment. "All clear, sir."

Zoe pushed open the door that led into the modest living room. She stepped inside and waited for him. "Welcome to my place." She rushed over to the radiator and grabbed some shirts and a black lacy bra. They'd been laid out to dry since clothes dryers weren't common in the region. "Sorry about the laundry." She moved the articles of clothing behind her back. "I wasn't expecting company."

"Don't worry. I'm the one who is intruding. I'll admit I've always wondered about your home life."

Her eyes widened. "You did?"

He nodded. "You always kept this part of your life such a mystery. I never even had the opportunity to meet your mother. I would have liked that. Maybe she could have told me some stories about you when you were a kid."

"She would have enjoyed that. Mum loved to tell stories."

He repeated Zoe's words in his mind. "You said that in the past tense." He stepped closer to her, wondering if he'd solved the reason for the smudges beneath Zoe's eyes and the pained look reflected in her eyes when she didn't think he was watching her. "Did something happen to your mother? Did…did she pass on?"

"What? No. Of course not."

"But the way you talked about her—"

"It was nothing. A slip of the tongue."

She snatched up a bed pillow from the old wooden framed couch with a yellow-and-blue-checked pattern. "It's my mother's. Sometimes she falls asleep out here."

"Will she be home soon?"

"Uh, no. She won't be home until the week of Christmas."

"I'm surprised you still live with her." He thought back to the numerous conversations they'd had when they were dating and how Zoe was anxious to move out on her own—that is until he swayed her to marry him. "What happened to your plan to get your own place—somewhere closer to the sea?"

"I…um, changed my mind." Her gaze lowered and her face took on a pale, pasty tone. "Let me put this laundry away, and then I can get you something to drink."

"No need." He didn't want to make her any more uncomfortable. "Go ahead and do what you need to. I'll be fine here."

"I…I'll be back with those sketches." She gave the area one last glance as though making sure everything was in its place before moving off down a hallway.

The apartment was tiny—much tinier than he'd been imagining. The living room consisted of a couch, a small white table for magazines and a simple wooden stand with an old television atop of it. The living area was directly connected to the kitchen. The space was one long, narrow room.

There was nothing fancy about any of it. Everything was clean, but almost everything had seen its better day. He never imagined that Zoe struggled to get by. When he saw her snappy clothes, he'd just assumed that she had a comfy life. But it looked like she, too, was a master of appearances.

He moved over to a group of framed pictures hanging behind the couch. There was one of Zoe as a little girl. She was so cute with her long braids. And there was another of her and who he assumed was her mother on the beach. Zoe looked so happy—so full of dreams. He wondered what happened to those dreams.

He turned around, taking in the white paint coating the wall behind the framed family photos. Even the kitchen was white except for the tan and aqua tiles serving as a backsplash. When he turned fully around he noticed the wall behind the television was anything but white. In fact, it was quite intriguing.

He stepped back against the couch to get a better look. It was a mural. Pastel colors blended to create a giant conch shell resting in the sand with the foamy sea in the background. Blue skies with a couple of puffy white clouds reached up to the ceiling. Wow!

He couldn't tear his gaze from this humongous masterpiece. Zoe was so much more talented than he'd ever imagined. What was she doing hiding her talent by sorting through paint chips and picking couches? She should be creating artwork for the world to enjoy.

"I've got it." Zoe rushed back into the room. "We can go now."

"Not so fast. When were you going to tell me about this?" He gestured to the wall.

She shrugged. "It's just something I did for my mother."

"Well, she's one lucky lady." He noticed Zoe's lack of response. He assumed that she was just being modest. "Don't be shy. Why aren't you painting full-time?"

Zoe's fine brows scrunched together as she shot him an

are-you-serious look. "Because painting doesn't pay the bills. I need a steady paycheck, especially now."

Now? What did that mean? There was definitely something he was missing and he fully intended to find out what. "Zoe, tell me what's going on with you. I know that you aren't telling me everything."

"I don't want to talk about it. I've got the sketches. Now we can go."

"No, we can't. I don't understand. Why won't you talk to me?"

"I am talking. And I'm telling you that if you want to get this mural done in time for the ball, I need to get started." She turned toward the door.

"Not so fast." He crossed his arms. "There's something I want to go over with you."

She sighed and then turned. "Does it have to be right now?"

"*Sì*." When she frowned, he continued. "I'd like you to walk me through exactly what happened with the annulment papers."

"I told you I signed them."

"And so far my advisors haven't found any trace of them. I thought since they were last seen here that this visit might jog your memory—something that you've forgotten."

Her mouth gaped open as pain reflected in her eyes. "You really think that I'd forget something that important?"

He raked his fingers through his hair. "I don't know what to think. That's the problem. You keep sidestepping things. Sometimes you stop in the middle of sentences and you leave me wondering what you're working so hard to hide from me."

"Why should I be hiding something?"

Frustration balled up inside him. He struggled to keep it at bay. "Because I was always able to read you before."

"You don't think I've changed since then?"

She was doing it again. She was dodging his questions by supplying questions of her own. "Zoe, stop with the questions. Just walk me through what happened to the annulment papers and the check."

Her gaze narrowed and her lips pressed into a firm line. Seconds passed and at last she spoke. "Fine. You want to know. Here it is. I had the papers. They were over there on the kitchen counter. I signed them. I put them in the envelope to drop in the mail. And then I ripped up your check into tiny pieces which I dropped in the garbage."

"Is it possible you accidentally dropped the papers in the garbage, too?" When she frowned at him, he said, "Okay. I just had to ask."

"I can assure you the check was the only thing I trashed."

"Why would you do that?"

"What? You don't think this place lives up to your standards and that I was foolish to toss away the money?"

"No, that isn't it." He clenched his jaw. He wasn't going to fall in that rabbit hole with her. What he needed to do was concentrate on the whereabouts of the annulment papers. "So you ripped up the check. What did you do with the papers? We need to make sure they didn't end up in the wrong hands."

"If they did, I didn't do it."

He believed her. It was highly doubtful, because by now he'd have been contacted for blackmail or it would have been sold to the paparazzi. Demetrius had a feeling the papers were right here in this apartment.

"Where did you last see the papers?"

"I…I don't know." Her shoulders slumped. "I've tried to remember ever since you told me they are missing, but I can't remember what I did with the envelope after I signed the papers."

"Think hard."

"I am. I must have posted it. That's the only reasonable explanation. They must have lost it."

"You didn't send it by special courier?"

She shook her head. "You have to believe me. I did what you wanted."

What he wanted? He never wanted this annulment. The only reason he'd issued the papers was because she'd walked out on him. He was about to say as much when he noticed her eyes grow shiny. Were those tears in her eyes? *Please don't start crying.* He was never good with women when they became emotional.

He moved to the counter. "Is this where you signed the papers?"

"*Sì.* That's the last place I remember having them." She paused as though she remembered something—something important. "I remember signing them and slipping them in the envelope. Then my phone rang. It was an important client."

"And?"

Zoe worried her bottom lip. Her gaze didn't meet his. "I had to go into the office early."

"Think hard about what you did with the papers."

Her eyes widened. "My mother offered to post them."

"Your mother? She knows about us? I thought you were waiting to tell her?" This could be a complication he hadn't anticipated.

"I swear I didn't tell her about us. She didn't have a clue what was in the envelope."

"So what do you think happened?"

"I think I know." Zoe rushed out of the room and down the hallway.

Demetrius followed. Zoe entered a small, modest bedroom. She stepped up to an old chest of drawers and

pulled open the top drawer. Frantically she started flip-
ping through papers and envelopes.

"Zoe, what are you doing?"

She didn't stop to look at him as her search continued.
"This is where my mother keeps her important papers."
Zoe grasped a large manila envelope and held it up. "It's
here."

Demetrius raked his fingers through his hair. A mix of
relief and worry rushed through him. Was he really supposed to believe her mother was hiding annulment papers
for a marriage that she wasn't supposed to know about?

Zoe smiled. "Isn't this great?"

"Great?"

"Yeah, you know, because no one else has the papers.
The media doesn't know. Your reputation as a reformed,
reliable prince is intact."

"Until you mother finds the papers missing and does
something about it."

"That won't happen. She couldn't tell anyone even if
she wanted to." There was a certainty in Zoe's voice, but
he wasn't so sure. He didn't even know her mother except
for what Zoe had told him about the woman.

"Why won't it happen?" When Zoe averted her gaze,
he stepped closer to her. "Zoe, stop with the cryptic comments. Tell me what is going on. I need to understand."

CHAPTER TWELVE

This was going to be the most difficult conversation of her life.

Where did she even start?

Demetrius stepped closer. "Zoe, whatever it is, just say it. I'm listening."

She glanced up, meeting his unwavering stare. Within his eyes she found a steadiness that she craved. She could do this. She would get through this confession just like she'd endured all of the doctors' visits, the testing and the trying times with her mother.

"It all started before you and I met. My mother started forgetting little things at first, like not going to the market. And then I started to notice her cooking had changed. Instead of the big, traditional meals, she would heat up ready-to-serve food. And sometimes it was burned. My mother never burned food in the past. She was amazing in the kitchen." Zoe blinked, keeping her tears at bay. "I didn't want to see what was happening to her, and she was so busy trying to cover up her lapses that she was too embarrassed to ask for help. So we both ignored the telltale signs—signs I didn't even know I should be watching for."

Demetrius reached out to her, but Zoe backed away. If she gave in to the tears now, she'd never get this out and she'd kept it bottled up for too long. He had to realize that a future with her wasn't possible. He already had an entire nation's troubles to handle. He didn't need hers, too.

She drew in an unsteady breath. "By the time I met you, my mother was no longer able to keep up with her job and was let go. That's when we couldn't ignore her problem any longer. The doctors told us it was Alzheimer's. But I was in denial. I couldn't accept that I am going to lose my mother one agonizing piece at a time until she no longer knows me." A sob caught in Zoe's throat. She choked it down. "My mother's going to forget everything."

"I had no idea."

"You weren't supposed to know. I couldn't cope with the diagnosis. The last thing I wanted was sympathy. I just wanted to pretend everything was normal."

"And I was the perfect distraction."

She nodded. "I let myself get swept up in the romance, and I did my best to block out the problems at home. I tried to keep everything as routine as possible. But as time went on, my mother's condition got harder and harder to ignore. When we were out with friends, my mother grew quiet and withdrawn, only talking when spoken to and answering with short, vague answers. Her gaze would dart around the group watching for other peoples' facial responses to certain comments and then she'd respond accordingly." Zoe blinked repeatedly. "I am watching my mother disappear and there's nothing I can do to stop it."

Sympathy reflected in Demetrius's eyes. "And the night you left the palace."

"That was the night that I could no longer ignore what was happening to her and by extension my life. That night she got lost and the *polizia* picked her up. She couldn't remember where she lived. Luckily, she remembered her name."

His voice was soft and soothing. "Why didn't you tell me?"

"Tell you what? That my mother needed me, and I didn't have time to be a princess?"

Demetrius frowned. "I'm being serious. I would have helped you."

"I know. And that's why I didn't tell you. I didn't want

you looking at me like you are now." She took off down the hallway.

He followed her to the living room where he stopped in front of her. "And how am I looking at you?"

She stared at the floor. "With pity in your eyes."

He placed a finger beneath her chin and lifted until their gazes met. "No, that's compassion you see. I can feel compassion, can't I?"

She shrugged, not exactly sure what to say.

"You shouldn't have to go through all of this alone."

The truth is she'd never felt more alone. Her gaze met his. She yearned to reach out to him, to feel his reassuring touch. Her fingers tingled, longing to slip around his hand—to feel that human connection.

She staved off the desire. "I...I'm not alone. I still have my mother."

He had never seen this coming.

Demetrius felt totally at a loss.

Witnessing Zoe's pain tore at him. He wanted to make it all better for her, but not even a prince could solve her misery. All he could do was let her know that he'd be there for her. Right now, he'd do almost anything for her.

She was, after all, his wife. Maybe they hadn't realized exactly what that meant when they'd made their vows, but he'd done a lot of reflecting since then. Being married meant being there for each other through the good and the bad. He wouldn't abandon her. She needed him, even if she refused to admit it.

He gazed deep into her eyes while feeling a tug in his gut. "And you've got me should you ever need a friend. After all, you're still my wife. My very amazing, compassionate wife."

"And you are still my husband." Her voice wobbled.

"Which gives me the right to do this." He pulled her

closer. She didn't resist as her hands came to rest upon his chest.

At last, he could do what he'd been thinking about since they'd kissed at the beach house. His hold on her tightened. Her hands slid up over his shoulders and wrapped around his neck.

His head dipped, seeking out her petal-soft lips. His mouth brushed over hers, sending a jolt of awareness zinging through his whole body. His heart ached for her and everything she'd endured on her own. He wanted her to know that she wasn't alone.

Her lips moved hungrily under his as her fingernails raked through his hair. Her soft curves pressed up against the length of him and a moan swelled deep in his throat. They'd been apart for far too long. He was still her husband, and he had every right to comfort his wife.

Their kiss grew in intensity and it no longer mattered that they were standing in the center of her living room. All that mattered is that they were together and they weren't arguing. They definitely weren't arguing. At last, they seemed to be on the right page and he wasn't about to let her go. Not now when he'd just got her back in his arms. There was plenty of time later to figure out where they went from here. It wasn't important now.

In the background there was a sound. He tried to listen but when Zoe caught his bottom lip between her teeth and sucked, his thoughts spiraled in a totally different direction. She was as turned on as he was. He moaned. It'd been so long—so very long.

There was that sound again. This time it was louder. And it didn't stop.

The annoying sound was a knock on the door, followed by someone calling out his name.

The moan in his throat turned to a groan of frustration. *Damn.*

With the greatest regret, he pulled back from Zoe. Her eyes fluttered open, showing her utter confusion. Her lips were rosy red and slightly swollen. And her cheeks were flushed. A smile pulled at his lips knowing that he was responsible for putting that freshly loved look on her face.

"I'll be right there." He called out to his bodyguard to keep him from intruding on his last few moments alone with Zoe. "I'm sorry. But we have to get moving, and I'm sure your neighbors will be relieved not to have my detail littering their hallways."

The disappointment was evident in her eyes and he hated that he couldn't erase it, but he had a job to do. There was always something that needed his attention. Since he'd assumed his proper role as crown prince, the constant meetings had never bothered him.

Those busy activities had been just what he'd needed after Zoe had left him. It had kept him from getting lost in his loneliness. The back-to-back meetings kept him from dwelling on where things had gone wrong in his brief marriage. But now, with Zoe back in his life, he wanted time to stop. He wanted to talk to her—to comfort her—to help her.

He scooped up the envelope with the annulment papers and then glanced at his watch. If they didn't get moving, he'd be late for his meeting with the king. And there was one part of the meeting that Demetrius was anticipating. At long last, he could tell the king and anyone else that cared to hear that their suspicions about Zoe were totally unfounded. His grip tightened on the papers. He was holding the proof in his hand.

While Zoe gathered her sketch pads and a few clothes, he pulled the papers from the envelope. They were indeed signed. This knowledge dampened his excitement over the passionate kiss they'd just shared. Zoe hadn't lied. She did indeed want out of their marriage. Disappointment settled heavy in his chest. There was still so much to discuss. He wasn't sure exactly what to do with the papers. For now, he would keep them safe.

"I'm ready." Zoe, wearing a pair of big black sunglass, came to a stop by the front door with a floral canvas bag slung over her shoulder. She lifted her hand and placed a pink ball cap on her head and eased her long ponytail through the opening in the back. "I wanted some stuff to wear for the times I walk on the beach."

He followed her out the door and down the steps. Once they were next to the car, Zoe came to an abrupt stop. Demetrius bumped into her. He instinctively reached for her shoulders to steady her.

"Zoe, what's the matter?"

Her head was turned to the right, staring down the alleyway. "Did you see that? There it is again."

He glanced around, not noticing anything out of the ordinary. "What is it?"

"A flash. Over there." She pointed between a couple of buildings across the street. "In the shadows."

Just because he hadn't seen it didn't mean it wasn't there. He nodded to the head of security who was standing by his side, hearing everything that was said. A couple of men took off to investigate.

Demetrius rushed her into the idling car. "Don't worry. You're safe."

He would do whatever it took to protect her. He remembered how they'd hounded his mother. She'd handled it with such grace—until that fatal day. On an outing, the paparazzi had gotten out of control, blocking the royal processional. And when his twin had grown bored and taken off into the crowd, mayhem had ensued. Security tried to move the paparazzi out of the way, but before they could a shot rang out. Demetrius's body stiffened at the memory of his mother being shot.

"Are you okay?" Zoe sent him a worried look.

"I'm fine." He patted her hand.

Whoever this stalker was, they'd find him before he did anything to Zoe. Demetrius vowed to keep her safe at all costs.

CHAPTER THIRTEEN

A VERY LONG day had passed and Zoe was still confused.

What does one say to the man who is officially your husband—an estranged husband at that—a prince—the man she'd made out with in the living room of the apartment she shared with her mother?

Well, the answer was simple. Nothing.

Or at least, as little as possible.

Not until she had her head screwed back on straight and her thoughts were actually coherent.

When Demetrius had dropped her off at the beach house the day before, she'd told him that she had a headache. It hadn't been a lie. Her head had ached from the constant tug-of-war between the will of her heart and the common sense of her mind.

She'd spent most of the night staring into the dark, trying to make sense of where things stood between her and Demetrius. Luckily, it was now Saturday and she didn't have to go to the office. She could spend the whole day at the beach house. She'd intended to complete her sketch for the mural, but she couldn't sit still long enough—especially not after Demetrius called to say he was stopping by because they needed to talk.

Talk? Talk about what? The South Shore project? Or the unforgettable kiss?

She glanced at the clock on the wall. A frown tugged at her mouth. It'd been almost two hours since he had called. Where was he?

As though in answer to her thoughts, there was a knock at the door. When it swung open, Demetrius strode in with a reserved look on his face. "Sorry I'm later than I planned. I had something to deal with."

"Uh, no problem." She wasn't about to admit that she'd been dying of curiosity to know what he wanted to discuss. A glance at the clock revealed that it was approaching lunchtime. "Would you like something to eat?"

"Before we get to that, I have something to show you." His face was devoid of emotion, but his voice held a serious note.

"Is something wrong?"

He paused as though trying to choose his words carefully. "Depends on how you look at it."

Her whole body tensed. "Quit dragging it out. Just tell me."

He pulled a folded piece of paper from his pocket and held it out to her. "This appeared in this morning's paper."

She hastily unfolded the clipping. There in color was a photo of her and Demetrius getting into his car outside her apartment building. The breath trapped in her lungs. Her mind raced with all of the ramifications.

"Zoe, relax. It's not as bad as you're thinking. Between your sunglasses, your cap and having your head lowered, no one can make out that it's you. Most of your face is hidden."

Zoe let out the pent-up breath. "What are we going to do?"

"Nothing."

"What? But we have to do something otherwise people will think—they'll think—"

"Nothing. There's nothing going on in the photo except I am helping someone into my car. Your name was not mentioned. Just a blurb about me being out and about in the city."

She turned to him, searching his face for answers. "This was taken by that creepy reporter, wasn't it?"

Demetrius rubbed the back of his neck. "That's my suspicion, but so far the paper is guarding their source. Don't worry. Now that you've moved in here, we shouldn't have any further problems with that photographer. But when we are out in public, we're going to have to be extra careful."

She nodded. "I understand."

He hesitated. Then deciding that he'd made his point, he changed the subject. "Now about lunch, I'll give the kitchen staff a call and have them send over something. What do you want?"

"Actually, I was thinking of making a salad." When he reached for his phone, she added, "You don't need to call anyone. The fridge is fully stocked. There's even some fresh shrimp."

"Sounds good." His facial expression said otherwise.

"If you want something else, that's fine."

He shook his head. "It's not the menu."

"Are you sure?"

He nodded. "It's just that I'm not exactly good in the kitchen. I haven't had much experience there."

"No problem. You can watch."

He started to roll up his sleeves. "And have you do all of the work? I don't think so. You just tell me what needs done and I'll do my best."

They moved to the kitchen and raided the refrigerator of all the fresh vegetables. Demetrius washed while she chopped. The truth was Zoe didn't have an appetite, no matter how colorful the vegetables or plump the already cooked shrimp.

Demetrius wasn't the problem—not exactly. It was what had happened a couple of nights ago that was bothering her. It'd be so easy to get caught up in more kisses, in more of this domestic bliss. But she knew the truth—the fact that she had a fifty-fifty chance of ending up like her mother. And she couldn't—wouldn't—put Demetrius through that. A sharp pain started in her finger and rushed up her arm.

"Hey, you're bleeding."

Zoe glanced down to see she'd nicked the tip of her thumb. She muttered under her breath as she moved to the sink to rinse it off.

"I'll get a bandage." Demetrius rushed out of the room. He quickly returned and played the concerned doctor as he applied antibiotic cream and a bandage. "Now sit down and I'll finish."

Grudgingly, she did as instructed.

He grabbed a tomato and started to slice it. "Were you able to work on your sketch?"

Really? He thought she'd be calm enough to be creative. "Umm...no."

"You know, I never did get to see any of your sketches. And you did say I'd get to choose one."

"And you will. But I don't want anyone seeing them until I do some more work on them." Cutting him off before he could launch into a rebuttal, she asked, "Did your meeting with the king go well?"

"It went as well as could be expected." Demetrius scraped the tomato pieces into the salad bowls. "I told him about all of your wonderful work at Residenza del Rosa. He's quite impressed. He'd like to meet with you some-time."

The king wanted to meet with her?

She didn't respond, not exactly sure what to say. She knew that she was supposed to be honored and tripping all over herself to accept, but her one and only encounter with the king had been anything but impressive. The king had been skeptical about her intentions as far as her mar-riage to his son.

The king had never insisted that she leave Demetrius, but he did make it clear if she were to stay what would be expected of her. He pointed out how she would be under constant scrutiny by the press. In her mind, all she could think about was her mother's disease being documented in the tabloids. How could she do that to her mother who was already struggling? And how could she do that to Demetrius?

"I don't think it'd be a good idea for us to meet."

"You worry too much. I told you I fixed things. He understands about the mix-up with the papers—"

"You told him about my mother?"

Demetrius stilled the knife and turned to her. "I wouldn't do that. I know how hard it was for you to tell me. When you're ready, you can tell people."

She breathed easier. *"Grazie."*

"You don't have to thank me. I wouldn't intentionally hurt you by breaking your trust."

But she was going to hurt him unless she cleared things up about the kiss. "Demetrius, we need to talk."

"I'm listening."

She took a deep, steadying breath, held it a second and then released it. "About yesterday—the kiss. It was a mistake." Was it her imagination or did his body tense? "It... it was an emotional moment for me and you were comforting me—"

"And things got out of control. Don't worry. I didn't read anything into it. That's actually what I wanted to talk to you about."

"You did?" When he nodded, she added, "So we're still good?"

There was a slight pause. "Don't worry. We're still friends. Now let's eat this amazing salad."

Knowing they were still friends should have made her feel better, but she couldn't help but think about what she was missing. Her gaze followed Demetrius as he carried their lunch to the table next to the windows. If only her life were different.

* * *

Just stay focused.

Zoe stifled a yawn.

Instead of reporting to her shared office at the palace each day, she now spent her days at the mansion. Piece by piece her vision for a relaxing atmosphere where family members would feel comfortable visiting with residents was coming together. When she wasn't pointing out where things went, she was painting her vision of a serene beach on the ballroom wall—the drawing Demetrius had finally settled on from her sketch pad.

However, Zoe had cut her day short and returned to the beach house. She'd thought of something she wanted to add to the mural, but she needed to do some research before she sketched it out.

For the umpteenth time, her fingers paused over the keyboard as her thoughts drifted away. Memories of the steamy lip-lock she'd shared with Demetrius played over and over. Even though they'd both agreed that it had been a mistake, she had a hard time defining that passionate, toe-curling kiss as a mistake. And she wanted more. Lots more.

The chirp of a bird out on the deck drew her out of her daydream. No matter how amazing that kiss had been, it couldn't be repeated. They were wrong for each other. After all, he was a royal prince bound by duty to produce the next healthy heir to the throne. And she, well, she was a mere commoner with no nobility in her past, no prestigious connections, nothing to offer the crown except some faulty genes.

Stirring up the burning embers between them would only lead to trouble.

The chimes of the doorbell rang through the beach house.

She rushed to the door. A smile lifted her lips in the

hope it'd be Demetrius. But he didn't normally ring the bell or wait to be greeted at the door. So who else could it be?

She swung open one of the expansive teal doors and there stood two uniformed men from the palace staff. Each held a cardboard box.

The older of the two men was the first to speak. "I believe you inquired about some extra Christmas decorations."

"I did. I want to surprise De—erm… Prince Demetrius. I thought he might enjoy a bit of holiday cheer."

When she'd passed the butler in the hallway the other day, she'd mentioned that the palace looked lovely. And she might have added that it'd be nice to have some of the extra decorations for the beach house. To be honest, she hadn't thought the man was paying her a bit of attention. Obviously he'd heard every word she'd said. She made a mental note to thank him.

"Where would you like these?" the younger man spoke up.

"I'll take them." She held out her arms for the box in his hands.

"It's okay, ma'am. We've got them. There are more in the truck—"

"More?"

"*Sì*. Lots more."

"Oh my. I didn't expect so much."

"You did ask for the extras, didn't you?"

"Um… I did. Come on in." She stepped out of their way. Luckily the beach house was quite spacious. "You can place them in the living room."

It took a few minutes for the two men to haul in boxes of all shapes and sizes. After Zoe saw the men off, she walked back into the living room and her mouth gaped open. What was Demetrius going to say when he saw all of this?

She smiled, thinking of the old Demetrius. He would

have thought it was great. He loved to find reasons to celebrate. He'd have popped some bubbly, turned on some festive music and been the first one to explore the boxes. Boy, she missed that part of him.

This new Demetrius had her stumped. She never knew what to expect from him. Just like that kiss that had come out of nowhere. What did it mean? Did it mean that he wanted them to start over? Or had it just been a fleeting thing?

Not wanting to dwell on those troubling thoughts any longer, she started opening boxes. There were ornaments, table decorations and wall hangings. But when she came to a pencil tree, she stopped. It was perfect. Now she just had to find a spot for it.

Zoe set to work. She placed the seven-foot Christmas tree next to the fireplace. The tree was adorable with a real bark trunk that was anchored in a red bucket. The short limbs were lined with white lights. All she had to do was plug it in. The twinkle lights lit up, sending a soft glow through the shadows now filling the room.

In another box, she found candles, which she lined along the mantel. After some digging in the kitchen, she found a lighter. With a chill in the air, she decided to go ahead and burn the logs in the fireplace. The apartment she shared with her mother didn't have such a luxury. And Zoe did love how the light from the fire danced upon the walls while the wood snapped and popped.

Onward she went digging through the boxes, amazed at the variety and quantity of decorations. No expense had been spared. She pulled out her cell phone and selected some Christmas music. She started singing along as she continued to create a holiday retreat.

"What's going on here?"

CHAPTER FOURTEEN

ZOE JUMPED, ALMOST dropping the glass ornament in her hand. She turned to find Demetrius propped against the wall. His arms were crossed while his facial expression was unreadable.

"I...I didn't hear you come in."

"Obviously. Do you want to explain all of this?"

Zoe retrieved her phone and switched off the music. "With Christmas just around the corner, I thought you might enjoy some holiday cheer."

"I had no idea that you planned to redecorate the beach house."

"I didn't. I mean, I'm not." She glanced down at the ornament in her hand. She turned to put it back in the box. So much for surprising him.

He glanced around. His gaze paused on the pile of boxes.

"Sorry about the mess. I'll make those boxes go away." Zoe worried, biting her bottom lip.

Demetrius turned to the fireplace. Now that the sun had sunk below the horizon, the flames of the fire flickered and cast a warm glow over the room. As the temperature rose, Demetrius discarded his suit jacket and rolled up the sleeves of his blue Oxford shirt.

Feeling a need to explain, she said, "I thought a fire would be nice."

He stepped up to the tree. He reached out and touched a glittery silver star ornament.

She swallowed hard, feeling like a kid with her hand in the proverbial cookie jar. "I can get rid of the tree, too."

When he turned, he was wearing that serious expression—the one that created lines between his brows. She laced her fingers together while wishing he would say something. She didn't deal well with the silent treatment.

Rushing to fill the awkward silence, she said, "I just got caught up in the excitement of the season. When I inquired at the palace about decorating, they sent over their extra ornaments. I never expected them to send so much stuff."

Demetrius glanced around at the opened boxes. "I think we need to do something about this."

In all honesty, it was rather a mess. It looked a little like Santa's workshop except instead of toys there were decorations. She really didn't want to take down the festive ornaments, but this wasn't her house. "I'll have everything put away tonight."

"Could you hand me that box?"

He was going to help her take down the tree? She thought of putting him off, hoping he'd change his mind. But she didn't want to push her luck. She quietly handed him the designated box. His fingers brushed over hers as he took it. Her pulse raced. Their gazes met but Zoe glanced away. Things were already complicated enough without making it worse.

In the silence where there once had been festive music, she started closing up the boxes. Perhaps she could fit them in a spare bedroom until she figured out exactly what to do with them.

"I could use a little help over here."

"Um. Sure." She closed the lid on another box before turning around. "What do you need?"

"You to help me." He waved her over to where he was standing near the Christmas tree. "Don't you think you've missed something?"

She was confused. "Oh, you want the tree taken down first?"

He shook his head. "That isn't what I mean. The tree is

only half-decorated. I think you better bring some more of those ornaments over here."

She stopped, her mouth gaping. He didn't want to take it all down? Instead, he was going to decorate the tree with her? Really? Maybe somewhere inside him there was still a little bit of the Demetrius she used to know—the one she'd fallen in love with.

A tempting thought crossed her mind. Would it be possible to find that smiling, fun-loving guy again? With a little bit of encouragement, would he let down his guard?

"Why are you looking at me like that?" His dark brows drew together. "Do I have a bit of garland or something in my hair?"

She smiled and shook her head. "Do you really want to help me decorate?"

He shrugged. "Why not? I'm always up for trying something different."

She grabbed the box with some ceramic ornaments. "You mean you've never decorated a Christmas tree before?"

"Not since I was a kid. Professional decorators come in to do the palace decorations. Everything has to be just right for photo ops."

She tried to envision a life where there were people that decorated your Christmas tree for you. It was so far from her modest lifestyle that it was a difficult concept. Right now, she didn't even have enough money to get her mother around-the-clock care.

"I guess when you're the richest man on the island, you can afford to have people do those sort of things for you."

He straightened. His shoulders took on a rigid line. He didn't say anything, but he didn't have to. She knew that she'd misspoken. She didn't mean anything by her comment. She'd just let her guard down and done some thinking out loud. She'd have to be careful going forward.

"I'm sorry. I didn't mean anything—"

"Could you hand me that candy cane ornament?" His gaze didn't meet hers.

"Um, sure." She moved to the couch.

She bent over to untangle the red ribbon looped around another ornament. After a bit of maneuvering, she freed it. She straightened and turned in time to find Demetrius staring at her. He quickly averted his eyes, but not before she realized that he was still attracted to her.

"Why don't you turn on the music you were playing when I interrupted you?" Demetrius hung the candy cane on the tree.

"You mean the Christmas carols?"

He nodded. "Then you can sing some more."

"Oh, no." Then she got an idea—a delicious idea. "Not unless you sing with me."

He waived off the idea. "I don't sing."

"Why not?"

He paused as though not quite sure. "It's not proper."

"Proper? Who's worried about proper? This is just you and me. And you know that I'm not proper most of the time. So let's hear it." She grabbed her phone and found the music app. With festive carols filling the silence between them, she sent him an expectant look. To her surprise and delight, his mouth started to move.

"I can't hear you." She grinned at him, excited to see the fun side of him. "Lip-synching doesn't count."

To her utter amazement and delight, he belted out a verse of "Santa Claus Is Coming to Town." Zoe clapped her hands. She hadn't had this much fun since...since Demetrius was a part of her life.

They added a variety of exquisite ornaments to the tree. None of them were like the common ornaments that Zoe and her mother hung on their little tree. These decorations were the best of the best. But then again, she supposed that was to be expected when they came from the royal palace—only the best for the king. Still, it felt weird to handle such valuable items.

As the evening progressed, they laughed and smiled more than they sang. At one point, they both took a few steps back to inspect their handiwork. Zoe loved their tree. Her gaze moved to Demetrius.

"Not too bad." He turned to look at her.

Unable to turn away, she added, "We do good work together."

He nodded. "My mother would have enjoyed this. She loved the beach house. It was her escape from the protocol of palace life." He strode over to the window overlooking the sea with the last bit of color in the darkening sky. "Did I ever tell you that my father built this house for her?"

"No. You didn't." Zoe glanced around the place, wondering what it'd be like to have someone love you enough to do all they could to make your dreams come true. Not that money and physical things can make a person happy. It's just the thought of the king going out of his way to make his queen happy was so romantic.

"My mother was the perfect queen. She was kind, thoughtful and beautiful. She was everything that my father could ever want. When the public was around she had the perfect smile, and when my brother and I were young, she made sure we looked and acted like the little princes the king could be proud of."

The love and awe was evident in Demetrius's voice. His love for his mother was as alive now as it had been all of those years ago. "She sounds amazing."

"She was. She would have liked you. I wish she'd have had a chance to meet you."

"I'm sure I would have liked her, too."

He turned around and glanced about the room. "She

would have loved what you've done with the beach house. Christmas was her favorite time of the year."

Zoe's gaze moved to the little tree that was still lacking something. She thought about it for a moment and then realized what was bothering her. "The angel is missing from the top of the tree."

"Grab it and we'll put it up there."

She rummaged through the boxes, finding the angel and something else—two tiny ceramic turtledoves. The artwork on them was quite detailed. She wondered if they were handmade.

"What else did you find?"

Zoe held out the ornaments, letting them dangle from the gold ribbon strung through each one. "Two turtledoves. My mother would love them." Zoe watched as the doves twisted back and forth. "They're her favorite birds as they represent true love since the birds mate for life."

"Really? I had no idea."

Zoe nodded. "When my father abandoned my mother, when she was pregnant with me—she lost her belief in love. She figured the only person she could count on was herself. But she said when I was born, she never felt such a strong love in her life. She said that with each smile, I healed her broken heart. She believed in love again...but sadly she's never found someone to share her life with."

"Don't look so sad. She has you. I'm sure watching you grow up made her very happy."

Zoe blinked repeatedly. "I guess you're right."

"Of course I am. I'm the prince." He smiled and winked at her, letting her see that lighthearted, teasing side of himself that she'd missed so much this past year. "Now, how about you find the perfect spot for those turtledoves while I put the angel on top?"

The best part of the evening was watching Demetrius let down his guard and enjoy helping her decorate. She glanced over as he climbed on a step stool to place the angel atop the tree. It was so easy to imagine that this was their first Christmas together as a real couple.

Just then he glanced over at her. Their gazes met and held. Her heart raced. She couldn't let herself get swept up in the moment. He smiled. This wasn't real. She smiled back.

Then again, there'd be enough time for reality tomorrow.

CHAPTER FIFTEEN

THIS WAS THE MOST amazing evening…ever.

Demetrius glanced over at Zoe. When they'd first been reunited on the mansion steps, he'd been prepared to despise the very ground she walked on. She was, after all, the woman who'd married him one day and then within forty-eight hours had ended their marriage. And now, he couldn't imagine holding such harsh feelings toward her.

Sure, she hadn't handled the situation with her mother very well, but he had no idea what he would have done if he'd been in her shoes. Maybe he'd been too caught up in his own problems with seeking his father's approval for his very hasty, very secretive wedding to notice her turmoil. Maybe if he'd made himself more accessible to Zoe, she might have turned to him—confided in him.

He'd never know. All they could do now was move forward. In the soft glow of the fire with the twinkle of the lights on the Christmas tree and festive lyrics filling the air, he couldn't be happier. And he had Zoe to thank for that. He glanced across the room, finding her busy organizing the empty boxes to be sent to storage.

As though she could sense him staring at her, she turned. Her gaze met his and she smiled, not a little smile but one that puffed up her cheeks and made her eyes sparkle like fine jewels. There was definitely no room here for anger or resentment over the past—not when her glowing smile filled him with such warmth.

If he could have one wish for Christmas, it would be this. Happiness, contentment and love—not that he had all of those things with Zoe. But maybe just for this one evening, he could pretend. After all, tomorrow would be soon enough for the sharp edges of life to pop their happy bubble.

He studied Zoe. What was so special about her?

Nothing.

Everything.

She had this way of disarming his strongest defenses and getting past his walls. Right now, when he looked at her as she sang some ridiculous Christmas tune, he no longer saw the woman who'd broken his heart, but rather he saw the woman who made his heart skip a beat or two with a mere touch or glance.

For a little while, he could have his one Christmas wish. Sure it was early in the year for presents, but maybe Christmas didn't have to occur on a certain day on the calendar. Maybe it was more about that special moment in one's heart when the pain and hurt melted away.

Maybe for tonight he could have what he wanted most of all—Zoe. When he was perfectly honest with himself, he'd never wanted to let her go. But after reading her note— seeing with his own eyes her desire to end their marriage, he'd had no choice but to accept the gut-wrenching fact that she didn't love him anymore.

Was it wrong to want to recapture a bit of the past? After all, at one point they had been happy. And they never did get to share Christmas together. They'd been cheated of one of the happiest times of the year. But not this year if he could help it.

"Hey, are you going to help me with these boxes before the palace staff shows up to haul them to storage?"

Zoe's voice snapped him out of his thoughts. "Sure. As long as you promise to share those chocolates."

"There are chocolates? Where?" Her whole face lit up. Then she started a mad search through the remainder of the boxes. She straightened with a triumphant look on her face. "And these aren't just any chocolates. They're the gourmet ones from Giovanni's Cioccolato."

Demetrius had to admit that he wasn't into chocolate, but he knew that it was one of Zoe's favorite indulgences. And Giovanni's was one of the finest chocolatiers in the Mediterranean. "Well, what are you waiting for?"

"Are you sure they meant to include them?"

"I might have mentioned they're your favorite."

"You did? Have I told you how amazing you are?"

"No, you haven't. Feel free to repeat that as many times as you like."

Right now, she could ask for the moon and he'd move heaven and earth to give it to her. He'd forgotten how powerful her smile was and how it radiated a warm, happy feeling within him.

Her fingers were a flurry of motion as she tore the wrapping paper from the box. Beneath the paper was a red ribbon, which she slipped off the maroon-and-gold box. And it wasn't a small box by any stretch of the imagination. Best of all was the look of excitement glinting in Zoe's eyes. If he had only remembered what joy chocolate brought to her, he would have had some ordered long ago.

She held out a chocolate to him. "Want some?"

"I'll have some later. Right now, I'll just watch you sample them."

"Are you sure?" When he nodded, she didn't waste any time slipping the chocolate between her raspberry-pink lips.

Demetrius couldn't help but stare as a look of ecstasy came over her. Zoe's eyes drifted shut in utter delight. The breath caught in his throat, unable to turn away from the sight of Zoe savoring the chocolate. When a moan of pleasure reached his ears, his heart slammed into his ribs. He definitely needed to buy this woman chocolate and often.

When her eyelids fluttered open, her gaze met his. The

tip of her tongue trailed over her lips. Her mouth lifted into a smile. She was doing this on purpose. His straining lungs insisted he blow out his pent-up breath. Blood pumped hard and fast through his veins. She had to know that she was driving him to utter distraction.

He watched her shimmery lips wrap around another piece of chocolate. This time, as she savored the candy, her gaze held his. Oh, she was a temptress. And it took every bit of willpower for him to keep his distance. But if he kept staring at her, he'd lose the battle. Second by second his common sense was slipping from his grip.

When she raised her fingers to her mouth, he intently watched. She popped one finger in her mouth. Her pink lips wrapped around it. Then she slowly withdrew it. A soft moan vibrated in his throat. Did she know just how crazy she was driving him?

She smiled at him. "That was amazing."

Indeed it was. Very much so.

"I suppose I need to finish with these boxes." Zoe re-placed the lid on the chocolates and set them aside. She moved back to the boxes.

Seriously? After all of that tempting and teasing, she was going back to work?

He glanced around at all of the decorations. If she could act indifferent, so could he. Though it might be the most difficult feat he'd ever accomplished.

Zoe tried to slow the rapid beat of her heart.

Being here with Demetrius in his bare feet, jeans and his shirtsleeves rolled up, it was so hard to remember that they were no longer a couple. But that was the way things had to be. It was best for Demetrius. Sucking down the sadness in knowing that she could never have the only man she'd ever loved, she got back to work straightening up the mess of boxes.

For a prince, he surprised her with the way he didn't complain about cleaning up. He even knew where the vacuum was kept, and to her astonishment he knew how to work it.

When everything was sorted, she turned to him. "*Grazie*. I didn't expect you to do all of this."

"I enjoyed this evening." He yawned and stretched.

His shirt rode up giving a hint of the light splattering of hair on his abdomen. Zoe inwardly groaned, unable to turn away. His gaze caught hers and it glittered with amusement. Heat flared in her cheeks. He'd busted her checking him out.

"I…I'm glad we could do it together." There was a nervous quiver in her stomach. "You should probably be going. I know you're tired and you probably have a lot of meetings first thing in the morning."

He took a step closer to her. "I know why you're trying to get rid of me—"

"I…I'm not." Liar. Liar.

"Zoe, you can't deny the chemistry between us. It's always been there." He moved until he was standing in front of her. "But there's one thing I need to know."

She gazed up into his eyes. Her heart squeezed. Not so long ago, when she looked into his eyes, she saw nothing but love. These days it was as if he had a protective wall around himself, and she couldn't tell what he was feeling. "What is that?"

When he spoke next his voice was soft and she had to strain to hear him. "Did you ever love me at all? Or was it all just a lie?"

The backs of her eyes stung. She blinked repeatedly. "How could you think that?"

"How could I not? You left me."

"It…it wasn't like that. You have to understand that it was such a difficult decision."

"But still you did it. You made the decision to leave." The walls came down and pain reflected in his eyes. All she wanted to do was soothe it away. He reached out, gripping her shoulders. "Please tell me. Did you love me?"

With each word spoken, it was getting harder and harder for her not to blurt out that she did love him—that she'd always loved him. She looked everywhere but at him. Her gaze came to rest on the French doors. They beckoned to her. "I…I never meant to hurt you."

"There's something else. Something that you're not saying. What is it?"

She shook her head.

"Zoe, look at me."

She didn't want to. How could she look him in the eyes and continue to deny that she still had feelings for him?

"Zoe, don't do this. Don't avoid talking to me because it's easier. Don't run away from us."

"I'm not running. I'm standing right here."

"And you can't even look at me. You might not be running down the beach, but inside you're hiding from your feelings—from being honest with me."

She faced him. "What do you want me to say?"

"I want you to tell me what you've been holding back all of this time. I want you to admit that we have something special and it isn't all in my imagination. I want this—" He swept her into his arms.

The surprise of his actions had her dazed for a moment. He pulled her close and without a moment's hesitation, his lips sought hers out. Her lips moved hungrily beneath his. This kiss wasn't sweet and innocent. His actions were full of raw emotions. Love. Loneliness. Pain. All jumbled together.

And what surprised her most was that she was just as hungry for him. For almost a year she longed for him. And this past month, he'd been so close and yet so far away.

What would it hurt if they shared this one special moment? They both wanted it—needed it.

Tonight they would create a memory to keep her company on the long, lonely nights when he was no longer hers. That was what this was—a passionate goodbye.

CHAPTER SIXTEEN

WHAT HAD HE DONE?

Demetrius raked his fingers through his hair as he lay back on the couch. Zoe's head rested against his bare chest. When this whole affair had begun, all he'd intended to do was get some answers from her and then negotiate an annulment that would keep their past out of the tabloids. When had he lost control?

Tonight he'd abandoned his resolve to hold her at arm's length. He'd tossed aside the walls he'd worked so hard to build between him and Zoe. When her lips had moved beneath his, none of the reasons he'd been telling himself to keep his distance from her seemed so important.

Nothing had mattered in that moment but being with her.

In the end, the joke was on him, because somewhere during that frantic kiss and their mind-blowing lovemaking he'd realized he wasn't over her. Not by a long shot. He loved Zoe as much today as he had the day he'd married her. Okay, a lot more.

But how was that possible?

How could he trust her when he knew that when times got tough she'd rather run than talk?

"What are you thinking?" Zoe's soft, dreamy voice wound its way through his alarming thoughts.

"The truth?"

"Always."

"I was wondering how we ended up here—like this."

Zoe pulled back and slipped on his discarded dress shirt. He liked the look on her. The shirt definitely looked so much better on her than it ever did on him. He'd never met anyone as beautiful as her—both inside and out. She was a very special woman.

Once she finished buttoning the shirt and rolling up the sleeves, she curled her bare legs up on the couch. She turned a big worried look to him and sighed. "Are you implying this was a mistake?"

He hated that he'd ruined this moment for her. He would have to be more careful with his words going forward. He reached out to her, but she resisted. He needed to say something to fix this. After all, it'd been a year since their marriage had failed. They'd both done a lot of growing up. This time, things would be different. "No, it wasn't a mistake. It was fantastic. You're fantastic."

At last, she gave in to the pull of his arms and snuggled to his side again. "I think you're fantastic, too."

His fingers stroked her silky hair. "You know, we still have to do something about the annulment?"

"I know. I just don't want to think about it tonight. I want one last night with you. A night where we don't have to think about the future."

He didn't like the thought that he'd never get to hold her like this again. He'd already been down that road. And even with his busy schedule and countless meetings, it still didn't erase the empty spot in his heart where Zoe should have been. But now she was back, and he didn't want to let her go again. Holding his wife close was heaven—it was the way it should be.

He cleared his throat. "Why does this have to be our last night together?"

"You know it would never work. Surely by now, you can see that our lives are too different. We've already talked about this."

He scooted over to the edge of the couch in order to actually be able to see her face. "No, we didn't talk about it. You always make excuses or skirt around the issue."

"I do not." She paused as though considering his words. "Okay, so maybe I do. It's not easy to talk about."

"The important things in life aren't normally easy, but that doesn't mean you should run from them."

She sighed. "I'm trying to do better—to take things head-on. I never thought about it before you mentioned it, but I guess I've got some of my father in me."

"You never talk about him."

"That's because there isn't much to say. My mother used to say he was a dabbler. He dabbled with this or dabbled with that until something bigger or better came along. And if things got too tough, he ran. When my mum got pregnant, he ran."

"I'm sorry."

Zoe shrugged. "It's okay. My mum was enough for me. But the one thing he did give me was my artistic ability. I have a painting in my bedroom that he did of the snow-capped Alps. It's the only thing of value that I got from him."

Demetrius liked that she was letting him in. At last, she was letting down her guard. He settled back on the couch next to her. Her cheek once again pressed to his chest. He wondered if she could hear how hard his heart was pounding.

She played with a loose thread on the shirtsleeve. "Would you still want me if I had a secret?"

His body stiffened. "What secret?"

"Relax." She pressed a hand to his chest. "We're talking hypothetically. You know, what if I had a criminal past?"

His muscles eased upon accepting that they were playing a game of what-if. "I don't know what it matters because you don't have a criminal past."

"But if I did, would you still care about me? Would you have still asked me to marry you?"

He wrapped a lock of her long dark hair around his finger. "Of course. How could I say no when you look at me with those big brown eyes of yours?"

"Demetrius, I'm being serious. I want you to be honest."

His jaw tightened. He didn't know where this conversation was going, but he suddenly didn't like the direction—not one little bit. "Fine. I don't know what I'd have done. I guess it would have all depended on the secret. If you're an ax murderer, then probably not. If it's something else, we'd face it—together."

"How can you say that? There's no way you can marry someone who isn't perfect—someone who would be a princess and eventually your queen."

He wanted to change the subject. This conversation was making him exceedingly uncomfortable. "Why don't we talk about the mural? Do you think you'll have enough time to finish it—"

"Demetrius, this is important. Don't change the subject."

"Fine. I don't know what I'd have done if you weren't perfect, but you are. So it's a moot point."

"But you don't know that. We didn't know each other that long when we eloped. What if you found out after we married that I couldn't have children? That I couldn't give you any heirs to the throne?"

His chest tightened. He never would have guessed this was what she'd been holding back. "You can't have kids?"

"I can...at least I think I can." Her hand slid up over his chest. "Relax. Remember this is just a round of what-if."

"I don't like this game." A frown pulled at his lips.

"Humor me. If you knew I couldn't have kids, would you have stuck by me?"

"Of course."

"Out of sympathy?"

"Stop. I'm done with this game. I knew everything I needed to know when I married you."

He tickled her side, knowing all of her sensitive spots.

He was tired of all this serious conversation. He wanted to see her smile again.

The corners of her mouth lifted, but she swiped away his hand. "I'm not talking about that. I'm serious. How did you know that marrying me wouldn't be a mistake?"

"Fine. If you want to know, I had you checked out. I might have been a little reckless back then, but I did have to be cautious."

She sprang up off the couch. The parts of his body where she'd been snuggled quickly grew cold. But the fire in her eyes practically singed him. "What do you mean you had me checked out? You mean you had people spying on me? How could you?"

"Of course I didn't have people following you around. But a standard background check was imperative, especially if we were going to make things formal. I don't know what you're getting so worked up about. They didn't uncover anything. You didn't even have so much as a motor vehicle violation."

"Of course I didn't. I don't own a car. Public transportation is so much easier. But that's beside the point. You violated my privacy."

"Why are you getting so worked up? I didn't do anything that the paparazzi wouldn't have done when they found out about you and me."

Her mouth gaped as though she hadn't realized how intrusive the paparazzi would be in her life. That creepy reporter would be nothing compared to the numerous exposés about any little bit of juicy information the press could dig up. And if they couldn't dig up any dirt, they'd create some—of that he was certain since they'd done it to him. Although to be honest, after his mother died and his father had withdrawn from his family, Demetrius had given the press plenty of fodder to fill their front pages. But Zoe didn't need to know any of that.

"And you didn't find out anything about me that would stop you from marrying me?" Her big eyes searched his.

"Of course not." Was she trying to tell him that there was something there—something that the palace staff had missed? "Tell me, Zoe. What should they have found? Is this about your mother?"

"No." The little bit of color in her face faded away. "Um…it's nothing. I'm just rambling."

He wanted to believe her. Honestly, he did. But there was still something she wasn't saying—something that she was afraid of him learning. Still, he didn't think it was as big of a deal as she was making it out to be. His staff may have missed something small—something inconsequential—but there was no way they'd have missed something that would affect the royal family.

CHAPTER SEVENTEEN

TWELVE DAYS.

Twelve very fast days had passed.

This amazing fairy tale was almost over.

Zoe started down the steps from the administrative offices of Residenza del Rosa. Perhaps she should smile because at last she'd secured her mother's safety and care. And she'd done it without involving Demetrius. She'd negotiated with the center's administrator to get her mother a room there. The administrator realized that Zoe had the prince's ear, but to her relief, he didn't make a big deal of it.

However, the administrator did make a big deal of her completed mural. He was exceedingly impressed with it as well as her interior design. He offered that in exchange for Zoe teaching art classes to the center's residents, she would get a reduced rate on her mother's care. Zoe immediately jumped at the offer. Even with the reduction, the cost would stretch Zoe's budget. However, she would do whatever it took to see that her mother had the care she needed. And this move would retain as much of her mother's dignity as possible. That was very important to her mother. And her mother's happiness was very important to Zoe.

She had reached the last step when she noticed Demetrius stroll past the reception desk. He wasn't alone. There was the female reporter, Carla Russo, next to him with a mic and a photographer in front of them. Demetrius's manner was casual as though he lived in front of the camera all of his life. Then again, he pretty much had lived out his life with a camera following him around. She could never imagine being at such ease with the press.

This interview must be another push for publicity for the revitalization project. Zoe hung back. She knew that he was keeping certain parts of Residenza del Rosa under wraps until the night of the Royal Christmas Ball—rooms such as the library, the garden and the ballroom.

As though Demetrius could sense her gaze on him, he turned her way. "And here is the mastermind behind the mural."

The photographer focused in on Zoe. The flash practically blinded her. What in the world? She wasn't prepared for this. She wasn't even dressed appropriately for photos. Her hair was pulled back in a haphazard fashion while her makeup was almost nonexistent. What was Demetrius thinking?

Ms. Russo smiled at her. "Hello again, Miss Sarris. We're very anxious to see your mural. Prince Demetrius says that it's a sight to behold."

Zoe's gaze moved to Demetrius. He did? He said that about her—erm…about her work?

He smiled and nodded. "Ms. Sarris, will you please show them your masterpiece?"

Masterpiece? Wasn't he laying it on a bit thick? After all, she definitely was no Leonardo da Vinci or Michelangelo. Not even close. She just did her best and hoped other people would take pleasure from her efforts.

Zoe swallowed hard. "I'm very honored that His Royal Highness has enjoyed my work. I just hope you're not disappointed."

"I'm sure we won't be." The eager look on Carla Russo's face revealed her true interest in Zoe's work. "Is it possible to see it now?"

Zoe's gaze sought out Demetrius. He'd moved into the background, leaving her alone in the spotlight. She had no idea what he was up to and no way of asking him privately. The only thing she did know was that he'd been super kind to her these past couple of weeks, reminding her of all the reasons she'd fallen in love with him in the first place.

When Demetrius nodded toward the ballroom, she knew that he was giving her yet another gift. Her heart gave a fluttering sensation as his gaze held hers. He was giving her a chance to spread her wings as an artist and to make a name for herself. How would she ever repay him?

She turned back to Ms. Russo. "The mural is right this way."

As they walked, the reporter asked one question after the next. "Was the mural your idea or was it something the prince came up with?"

"Um…it was actually my idea. I wanted to give the residents a relaxing, calming atmosphere. My mother has a great love of the sea, having grown up in a seaside village. I recently painted a similar mural for her. Though not nearly as large, she has enjoyed it a lot. And…and I thought others might enjoy it, too." Zoe wondered if it was a mistake mentioning her mother, but it was too late to worry about it now.

"Your mother is one very lucky lady to have an artist for a daughter." Ms. Russo meant well, but her words dug at the tender spot on Zoe's heart.

"I've been fortunate enough to view both murals and they are amazing," interjected Demetrius. "We were very lucky to have Ms. Sarris sign on for this project. She's very talented."

"And has it been decided if she'll be working on the other buildings slated for renovation?" Ms. Russo held out the digital voice recorder for him to speak into.

Demetrius's gaze met Zoe's before turning back to the reporter. "That's my hope, but we're currently in negotiations."

He didn't disclose anything in his facial expression, but Zoe could tell he wasn't referring to the revitalization project any longer. Her heart fluttered. Try as she might, she just couldn't get him out of her system—even if it was the only way to protect him from his own good intentions.

When he found out about her chance of inheriting her mother's disease, he would stay with her for all of the wrong reasons—pity, obligation and honor. She couldn't let him fall on his sword for her. She loved him too much for that.

Ms. Russo turned to Zoe. "When Prince Demetrius called to tell me about your mural, he couldn't stop singing your praises. You've definitely won him over, which I hear isn't an easy feat."

"We should move along. Ms. Sarris's time is limited." Demetrius stepped up to Zoe's side. "She still has a lot of final touches to attend to before the ball."

Ms. Russo frowned, but she quietly continued toward the ballroom. When the reporter turned away, Zoe could at last take in a full breath of air. She turned to him and flashed him a grateful smile.

He smiled back and signaled for her to lead the way to the mural. After weeks of hammering, plastering and painting, it was time for the grand reveal of Residenza del Rosa. On shaky legs, Zoe moved into the lead.

Even Demetrius had yet to see the mural since she'd put the final touches on it. All it needed now was a clear topcoat to help keep the colors from fading as well as to protect it from fingerprints. She'd been worried about how it would be received, but now with Demetrius's encouragement and the administrator's praises, she felt confident enough to share it with others.

She swung the door to the ballroom open and stood back, letting the others enter. The reporter and the photographer rushed forward, but Demetrius hung back, refusing to enter until Zoe had done so. He was forever a gentleman. That was just one of the many things she loved about him. The truth was there was so much to love about him that if she wasn't careful, she was going to throw caution to the wind and forget why this relationship couldn't be a forever thing.

The small group stopped in front of the mural. Her stomach quivered with nerves. She gazed up at her greatest creation and hoped it would be well received. Her gaze settled on the deepening blue sky dotted with puffy white clouds. Midway down was the bright orange and yellow of the sun as it started its descent into the horizon. Brilliant shades of orange, pink and purple streaked out along the sea. The calmness of the dark blue water reflected the sun's rays as the tide gently rolled into a sandy shore. Upon the beach rested a maroon sailboat with a yellow stripe. She'd wanted to give the impression that it was waiting for someone to sail away in it—away from their troubles—to a place of peace and tranquility.

After answering countless questions, more about what it was like to work with the prince than her artwork or her interior design work, Ms. Russo and the photographer departed. Zoe sighed in relief. At last her lungs could fully expand as her tense muscles loosened up. She would definitely not make a good spokesperson like Annabelle. Not a chance.

Zoe turned to him. "I wish you'd have given a little warning about the interview. I'm a mess." She ran a hand over her hair. "Those pictures are going to be terrible."

"They will be beautiful, just like you." His gaze met and held hers.

Her heart pit-pattered faster.

"I don't know how you deal with the press day in and day out."

Demetrius walked over and opened the door leading to the veranda. "In all honesty, I don't like answering questions, but it's part of my world. I guess for the most part, I've grown used to it—at least as much as anyone can."

She followed him outside. "I want to thank you for this

amazing opportunity, but words don't seem like enough. I still can't believe you went to all of this bother for me."

"What bother?" He acted so innocent, but she knew he went out of his way just for her. "Oh, you mean arranging for Residenza del Rosa to get some additional coverage? I should be the one thanking you."

She shook her head. "Don't dismiss this. Admit it. This wasn't about the center. You didn't even mention it."

His dark brows scrunched together. "I didn't? Surely I must have."

She couldn't help but smile at his antics. "Afraid not. Maybe if you run after them, you can catch them."

"Hmm… I don't think so. I'd rather stay here." He gazed deeply into her eyes.

"You would?" Her voice came out much softer and sultrier than she'd intended.

He nodded, stepping closer.

"I don't know why you did what you did today, but *grazie*. You don't know what this means to me."

His hand slipped around her waist. "Does this mean that you're not upset about the impromptu interview?"

She lifted onto her tiptoes and leaned forward. "If I was mad, would I do this?"

Her lips met his. At first, he didn't move as though he were afraid of scaring her away. She slipped her arms up over his shoulders and moved her mouth over his. That's all it took for him to reach out and pull her close.

Her heart swelled with love. She knew that this thing— them together—couldn't last forever, but in that moment, it didn't matter. No one had ever done something so sweet, so thoughtful for her.

She reveled in the fact that he wanted her as much as she wanted him. The kiss went on and on. She didn't want it to end. She knew when it did that they'd crash back into reality. And indulging in a passionate kiss with the Crown

Prince of Mirraccino was not part of her reality—even if they were secretly married.

The sound of footsteps caused them to spring apart. Her gaze met his and she knew that if they'd been back at the beach house things wouldn't have ended there. And if she was honest, she didn't want it to end. The more of Demetrius she had, the more she wanted.

He straightened his shirt. "I'll go inside and see who that is."

"I'm going to stay out here for a moment." She just needed a second or two alone to gather her thoughts.

He gave her a quick kiss and walked away.

A deep sadness replaced the joy in her heart because she knew that just like Cinderella, when the ball was over, she would turn back into a pumpkin. Her life and that of the prince wouldn't—couldn't—intersect again.

The next evening, Demetrius's shoulders sagged.

He was exhausted.

And now he had to do something that would only succeed in upsetting Zoe. He clutched the day's newspaper in his hand as he knocked on the door. Accustomed to coming and going without any formality, he let himself inside.

He was immediately greeted by the most delicious aroma of butter and sugar. Was Zoe baking? His steps came a little quicker as he made a beeline for the kitchen.

Sure enough, Zoe was pulling a tray of cookies from the oven. She glanced in his direction and smiled. "You're just in time to help."

"Help? With what?" He sure hoped she didn't want him to bake anything. It'd end up burnt to a crisp. He sat down on a stool at the kitchen island and tossed the paper on a neighboring stool.

She slid another tray in the oven before turning to him. "Don't look so worried."

"What are all of the cookies for?" He'd never seen so many cookies decked out in red, white and green sprinkles.

"I thought I'd do something special for the workers at the mansion. They've really gone out of their way to make this whole project a success." Worry lines creased her beautiful face as she looked around the kitchen at the dozens of sugar cookies. "Do you think it's a silly idea?"

"Silly? Absolutely not. In fact, I'm jealous."

"No, you're not."

"Oh, but I am. In all the time I've known you, you've never baked me cookies."

"I did too." She paused as though searching her memories. "Didn't I? Surely I must have."

He shook his head, knowing he was right. He'd never forget having such a pretty young lady present him with homemade cookies.

"Hmm..." Her lips pressed into a firm line. "Well, maybe you won't even like them."

"Why don't you pass me one and I'll let you know."

She snatched up one in the shape of Santa with red and white sprinkles. She held it just out of his reach. "You can have it on one condition."

He arched a brow. "What would that be?"

"You help me decorate the rest."

He glanced at the two trays of bare cookies, then at the almost empty mixing bowl and at last he focused on that cookie in her hand—that very tempting cookie. "Okay, you've got a deal. Just don't expect them to be pretty like yours."

"Just do your best." She placed the cookie in his hand.

Their fingertips brushed and a current of awareness zinged up his arm. Suddenly, he didn't feel so tired. He eyed up Zoe, who was smiling at him. "Pass me one of those trays and some sprinkles."

"Not before you wash up."

"Of course." He returned her smile. The action felt so strange after he'd frowned most of the day.

For the next hour, they worked together on the cookies. He got in trouble numerous times for thieving one or two. He couldn't help it. They were the best he'd ever tasted. And it didn't hurt that the baker looked pretty tasty, too. Her pink lips beckoned to him.

"Hey, mister, you're supposed to be working."

"I'm done." He pushed the decorated cookies across the counter. "And now I take my payment in kisses."

She laughed. "I don't seem to recall that."

"Well come over here and I'll remind you."

She smiled and shook her head. "You come over here."

The invitation was too good to resist. He got to his feet and rounded the counter. When he stood in front of her eagerly anticipating her cookie-sweet kisses, she instead tossed him a dishcloth before turning to the sink full of dishes.

A frown tugged at his lips. "What about those kisses you owe me."

"You don't get paid until the job is done."

"That's not fair."

She lifted up on her tiptoes and planted a kiss on his lips. But alas it was far too short. Her twinkling eyes stared at him, promising more. "Consider that a down payment."

"Well, what are you waiting for? Let's get those dishes done."

An hour or so later, Zoe closed the lid on the last storage container of cookies. "Everything is boxed up and ready to go in the morning." She walked over to the couch next to the lit Christmas tree. She stretched. "*Grazie*. I wouldn't have made it through those last trays on my own."

"Glad I could help, but I think I ate as many as I decorated." He rubbed his full stomach.

She laughed. "I think you're right."

There was no point in putting off his news any longer. This concerned her as much as it did him. "Zoe, we need to talk."

The smile faded from her face. "Any time you say those words, whatever follows is never good."

He wanted to tell her not to worry, but he knew that it would be futile. He might as well get this over as quickly as possible. He retrieved the newspaper from the stool in the kitchen.

"You need to see this" He handed over the paper.

She held it in front of her. A gasp filled the air. A color photo of them kissing made the headline of the *Mirraccino Gazzetta*. This wasn't the innocent peck under the mistletoe. This was a full-on, passionate embrace and lip-lock.

When he'd been roused from his bed in the middle of the night because an informant had delivered an advance copy, Demetrius hadn't wanted to read the accompanying blurb. But it was like a train crash that you just couldn't turn away from. His gaze had panned down to the words...

THE CROWN PRINCE IS SMITTEN!
Prince Demetrius and the interior designer Zoe Sarris are creating a steamy scene of their own.
Is the Prince going back to his old partying ways? Or has Ms. Sarris stolen his heart?
You be the judge.

Zoe's pale face turned to him. "But how?"

"Apparently a photographer snuck onto the terrace at Residenza del Rosa yesterday without anyone noticing. It seems that we put on quite a show for him."

Her worried gaze moved to him. "Do...do you know who the photographer is?"

"Not at this point. The security cameras aren't hooked up yet."

"Was it that creepy reporter who has been lurking about?"

"I don't know. My men are working on it."

"So everyone has seen this." Her face turned a pasty white. She jumped to her feet. "I need to tell my mother."

"Calm down. No one has seen this. At least not the general public. The palace staff took great pains to get the print run stopped and the story replaced."

She pressed a hand to her chest and breathed out. "Maybe you should have led with that part."

"The thing is, people know about us. There's no putting this genie back in the bottle—"

"But the palace staff—"

"Only delayed the inevitable. They gave us time to figure out how to spin the story."

"Spin it?" Worry lines marred her face.

He knew this was a lot for her to take in at once, but they didn't have much time to figure out what they were going to tell the public. He'd already decided what he wanted. He swallowed hard, hoping she'd agree. "I think we should announce our marriage."

"What? No." She shook her head. "You can't. You've worked so hard to redo your public image."

"And if this news comes from you and me, people will be happy for us. They'll all want to know how soon we'll be having children."

"Children?" Zoe looked as though she was going to pass out.

He hadn't meant to throw everything at her at once. "It's okay. We can wait. There's no rush."

"The king…he won't be happy if we reconcile. Not at all. He wasn't pleased when you brought me home the first time."

"That's because I caught him off guard. This is different."

When her mouth opened again, he pressed a finger to her lips. "Don't say anything you'll regret. I know this comes as a big surprise. Think on it tonight and let me know tomorrow." He paused and though it pained him to say it, he added, "I'll accept whatever decision you make, as long as you think about it. Will you do that for me?"

She grabbed his finger and gave a squeeze. "I will."

CHAPTER EIGHTEEN

HE WAS LATE.

Zoe checked her watch again. What was keeping Demetrius? It was his idea to meet here in the courtyard. Before he'd left the beach house last night, he'd made her promise that she'd give him an answer about what to tell the press regarding their relationship.

She hadn't slept a wink last night. Not that she had anything to debate. She had to walk away—she had to do what was best for Demetrius. The last thing he needed was to have a country to run and a wife with Alzheimer's. She'd stared into the dark, thinking how much she'd miss him. This time walking away would be so much harder. Her heart already ached.

Footsteps behind her had her turning. "Demetrius, I'm over here."

The smile slipped from her face when the creepy reporter stepped out from behind a lush shrub. Uneasiness inched down her spine. What was he doing here? What did he want with her?

"Ms. Sarris, at last we meet again." His leering smile revealed stained teeth.

Zoe didn't say anything as her eyes darted around searching for Demetrius or any of his security detail. There was no one about. Her palms broke out in a cold sweat as the hairs on her arms stood on end. She was alone with this man who was standing between her and the door. Why was he stalking her? What did he want with her?

"Excuse me. I'm needed inside." She attempted to go around him.

"Not so fast." The man in a white polo shirt and a blue sports jacket stepped in her way. "Don't worry. I'm not going to hurt you. See, you and I, we're going to become good friends."

Zoe, in an attempt to keep the man from touching her, stepped back so quickly that her foot landed on the edge of the walkway. She stumbled. Her arms flailed as she struggled to regain her balance.

"Careful." He clicked his tongue. "We don't want you getting hurt."

Her gaze hesitantly met his. "I have to go. People will be looking for me."

He shook his head. "You aren't going anywhere until we talk."

"What...what do you want from me?"

"I want the truth, Ms. Sarris. Or do you go by Princess Zoe now?"

Her heart hammered in her chest. He knew the truth. How could he? Was he just fishing? If he did know, what did he plan to do with the information? And if he knew this much, what did he want with her?

"Answer me!" His voice echoed off the surrounding walls.

"What? Uh...no. I'm just Zoe Sarris. A nobody."

The man's beady eyes narrowed. "Come now. You surely didn't think the prince was going to keep your secret forever."

"I...I don't know what you're talking about."

"Don't play dumb with me." His face filled with color. "I'm warning you. This is my big break and you aren't going to ruin it for me."

"I...I won't." Her gaze darted between him and the door. There was only one way out of the courtyard and it was straight past him.

The wild look in the man's eyes shook her to the core. She had to get out of there. Now!

She set off running. She pushed him out of her way, but he was too quick for her. His meaty fingers bit into the tender flesh of her upper arm. She let out a scream.

He yanked her to him and placed his other hand over her mouth. His voice was menacing as his hot breath brushed over her cheek, making her sick to her stomach. "That wasn't very nice of you." She yanked at his hand, but he was too strong for her. "I thought we could have a friendly conversation. Now, why did you have to go and ruin it?"

Zoe struggled to calm herself. Her gaze searched the doorway, willing Demetrius to appear. Where was he?

The man's bad breath smelled of garlic and onions. "If I let you go, do you promise to be quiet and not run?"

She nodded while swallowing hard to keep her nausea at bay.

First, he removed his hand from her mouth. She sucked in a deep breath. Next, he released her arm. She didn't move, not yet.

"Good. I knew you'd cooperate. Now, we were talking about your new title of princess. You know these sorts of things shouldn't be kept from the public."

"What...what do you mean?"

The man's beady eyes narrowed. "Did you honestly think I wouldn't do some digging into your life?"

"I don't know what you mean." Her gaze moved to the doorway. If only she had something to throw at him—just enough of a distraction to get past him.

"You aren't getting away. Not yet."

She hated that he knew what she was thinking. It was time for a different tactic. No matter that her insides shivered with fear, she had to stand up to this guy. She dug deep for a bit of confidence, hoping to bluff this man until

Demetrius showed up or she figured out a plan to get out of there.

She pressed her shaking hands to her hips, lifted her chin and prayed her voice wouldn't betray her. "What do you want from me?"

His eyes lit with surprise. "That's more like it, Princess. I've seen your marriage license. I know that you and Prince Demetrius tied the knot."

"If you know that, what do you need with me?"

"The thing is, even though I paid the clerk good money to browse through his records, I was interrupted. Before I could snap a photo, I had to sneak away."

"That sounds like your problem, not mine."

The man's eyes narrowed and his voice lowered. "It's your problem now because I want a confession." He held out a voice recorder. "I want you to tell the world that Prince Demetrius, heir to the throne of Mirraccino, has been sneaking around behind everyone's back with you. Does the king even know what his son has been up to?"

"What are you implying?"

"The readers have a right to know." He stepped up to her, cupping her chin with his hand. "Don't try to lie your way out of this. I already know the truth."

"I...I won't." She knocked his hand away. Her skin began to crawl where he'd touched her. "You already know everything, why do you need my confession?"

He swore under his breath. "Without concrete evidence, no paper will touch this story, not when it involves nobility. No one wants to be on the wrong side of the king. But with your verbal confession, they'll be able to verify your voice with that television interview you gave for that revitalization project. At last I'll be able to name my price. I'll be able to live a rich life like all of these people that I've had to report on—those people who don't even know I exist. That will all change once this story breaks."

"If all you want is money, Prince Demetrius will pay you—"

"It isn't all I want! Haven't you been listening? This story is going to be huge—it will be award winning. I'll be famous and rich. You wouldn't begrudge me my moment in the spotlight, would you?"

She shook her head vigorously.

The tension in his face eased. "You know, I've been watching you this past month—getting to know you. You're a good person. Much too good for the likes of that playboy prince."

As the man rambled on, she couldn't help but think this guy had it all turned around. She was the one who was damaged goods, not Demetrius. But she wasn't going to argue with this man. He'd obviously lost a firm grip on reality.

"So, now you will confess that you are in fact married to Prince Demetrius." He held the voice recorder up to her. Her gaze darted to the door. "Don't try running again. You won't like what happens if you do." The man patted his pocket as though he were armed. "You're not getting away this time."

Demetrius's body tensed.

He took in the scene unfolding in front of him. The wide-eyed fear written all over Zoe's face and the short, stout man leering at her.

So this was who'd been stalking Zoe. Well, no more. Anger drowned out any other thought of protocol. Demetrius rushed forth. When the stalker turned, Demetrius's clenched hand connected with the man's jaw. The man went down to the ground in a heap.

Zoe let out a scream. The security detail that Demetrius had ordered to remain at the doorway so he could speak to Zoe in private came rushing into the garden.

Once the stalker was detained, Demetrius rushed over

to Zoe. He reached out to her. Her body trembled as he pulled her to him.

"It's okay. You're safe now."

His arms wrapped tightly around her. He pressed her head to his chest. He hadn't been that scared since—since his mother had been shot. He closed his eyes, willing away the painful memories.

"I have a right to be here!" the man yelled. "The people have a right to know what their future ruler is up to with his supposed interior designer. Care to add a comment about your secret marriage?"

"Take him away," Demetrius called out. "Charge him with everything you can think of."

The men moved toward the door with the reporter fighting them. "What? You don't have a comment. Too bad. This is all going to come out. You can't hide."

Once the man was gone, Zoe pulled away from Demetrius. When he reached out to her again, she said, "Don't."

"Zoe, relax. You're safe now."

She wrapped her arms around herself and shook her head. "This—you and I—we...we aren't going to work. I can't do this."

Her words struck like daggers to his heart. "You're wrong. This time around will be different, I'm different."

"But I'm not. I can't have my life on display for the world."

"You're in shock. You don't know what you're saying—"

"I'm speaking the truth." Her voice was eerily calm. "I can't be the kind of princess you need—you deserve."

Her words stopped him from reaching out to her. Through all of this, he hadn't stopped to consider what he'd been asking of her. Asking her to remain his princess would put her whole life under the media's microscope. They wouldn't leave any stone in her life unturned—including her mother's illness.

In the end, the title of princess would bring her more pain than joy. He couldn't—wouldn't—do that to her.

Though the thought of walking away from her killed him, he had to do it. He loved her so much that he couldn't risk letting anything happen to her like what had happened to his mother. He'd vowed to protect Zoe, no matter what it cost him.

Besides, Zoe already had more than enough issues with her ailing mother. He couldn't put it off. He had to walk away now—before he lost his nerve. With a heavy heart, he started for the exit.

He paused at the doorway. He couldn't bring himself to turn around and see the pain swimming in her eyes. Instead he called out, "I'm sorry. My security will see that you get home safely."

Tonight he wouldn't sleep. Tonight he needed a long run on the beach. A chance to pull himself together—to figure out how he was once again going to let go of the woman he loved.

CHAPTER NINETEEN

SUMMONED TO THE PALACE.

This couldn't be good.

What did the king want to speak to her about? The incident yesterday with the stalker? Or was this meeting about the prince? Did the king want an assurance from her that she'd go away quietly once the ball was over?

Zoe's stomach quivered as the butler guided her through the grand entryway that was bigger than the entire apartment she shared with her mother. Instead of going to the left toward the offices, she was guided to the right. The staccato sound of her heels over the polished marble floor echoed against the ornate walls. She found her mouth gaping open in awe at such beauty.

As she made her way down a wide hallway, it was impossible not to gawk at the stunning artwork. Classic paintings hung on the wall between each doorway. There were also a handful of sculptures on pedestals. She was drawn to one such sculpture of a mother and her child. Zoe was struck by the emotion on the mother's face. Sadness assailed Zoe that she would never know such happiness while holding Demetrius's child.

Noticing that the butler had kept moving, she rushed to catch up. She couldn't even imagine what it was like to live there. It was like a museum. At the end of the impressive hallway were French doors that the butler swung open and then stood aside for her to pass by him. She glanced around at the enormous veranda with enough lawn furniture to easily accommodate a large luncheon party, but today the area was deserted, which seemed a shame on such a sunny day.

Though the last thing in the world Zoe felt like doing was partying. Right now, all she wanted to do was get as far from here as possible. So if the king had called her here to kick her out, he need not have wasted his time. She'd already moved back to her apartment.

"His Majesty is this way." For a man of his advanced years, the butler was surprisingly spry. He set off at a brisk pace down one of the many meandering paths in the sprawling garden.

As impressive as the interior of the palace was, she found the gardens utterly breathtaking. Geometrically shaped hedges surrounded each section. Within each section, there was just one vibrant color whether it was a flower, a fruit or a vegetable. It was awe inspiring. This whole place was a true treasure, in every sense of the word.

The butler came to a stop. "Your Majesty, Ms. Zoe Sarris."

She wasn't quite sure how to greet the king as their one and only meeting had been strained at best. This time things weren't much different. They really needed to stop meeting like this.

For the lack of an alternative, she did a quick curtsy and waited until the king spoke first. "May I call you Zoe?"

She nodded, too nervous to speak.

"Zoe, thanks for coming. Please walk with me." She nodded and moved to his side. "I heard about your unfortunate encounter yesterday. I'm sorry that happened. Are you okay? Is there anything you need?"

Other than a bandage for her broken heart, there wasn't much anyone could do. "I…I'm fine."

The king sent her a speculative look, but he didn't say anything else about the incident. "My wife loved the garden. She'd spend a lot of time out here. She said that everyone should pause to smell the roses…and often."

"She…she must have been quite a lady."

"She was. I miss her dearly. She was so much better at handling our boys than I have ever been. I've made so many mistakes along the way."

Zoe wasn't sure what to make of this conversation. She laced her fingers together to keep from fidgeting. Was he trying to apologize? Or was he preparing to send her packing? She really hoped it was the latter. It'd make leaving so much easier. Not that any part of this was easy.

The king stopped walking and turned to her. "I have a question for you." When she went to say something, he held up his hand, silencing her. "But I need you to think carefully and tell the truth. Can you do that?"

She didn't want to. She had a feeling she knew what his question was going to be. And the answer was best left unspoken. But she nodded her head anyway.

"Do you love my son?"

She was right about the question. The truth was Demetrius's name was tattooed upon her heart. She didn't know where the king was going with this conversation, but she couldn't lie. Not about that.

She nodded. "I love him. I never stopped."

The king didn't look the least bit surprised. "I suspected as much. And so will anyone who sees that picture of you two."

"But—"

He held up his hand again. "I need you to listen carefully to me."

She wrung her hands together. If only the king knew the whole truth, he would banish her from the palace—banish her from his son. Guilt hung heavy on her shoulders.

"I've watched my son over this past year. I've seen how he's grown—how he's taken on his responsibilities. And I couldn't be more proud of him. But this change came at a horrendous price."

Zoe's chest tightened. She knew that the king was going to blame her for his son's unhappiness. But he was too late. She already blamed herself. If she could undo it, she would.

The king's gaze met hers. "When he first brought you home, I didn't believe my son had found his soul mate. Back then he was known for his rash decisions. And I must admit that I was quite leery at first. I thought that his elopement was just him acting out again. But I was wrong. Over this past year I've learned how much he truly loves you."

Zoe blinked repeatedly, keeping her tears at bay. "I never meant to hurt him."

"I know, my dear. And I've called you here because I owe you an apology. If I have played a part in keeping you two apart, I am sorry. Please excuse this old man's meddling. I only ever wanted what was best for both of my sons."

Zoe couldn't let the king believe he was the reason for her and Demetrius breaking up. Sure, at first she was overwhelmed and a bit intimidated with the skepticism from the king and his advisors, but that was to be expected. Her problem was that she had unrealistic expectations—hopes that life with a prince would solve all of her problems.

The truth was only she could solve her problems—by facing them head-on. And even then there weren't always solutions, sometimes there was only acceptance of the inevitable.

"Your son is a wonderful man. He will one day be a great leader."

"But will you be by his side?"

The backs of her eyes stung with unshed tears. She shook her head. "It's better this way."

"My dear, if I've learned anything in this life, it is that life is fleeting and true love should never be taken for granted. If you love my son as you say you do, trust in him and his love."

She wanted to do just that, but the king had no idea what he was asking. He didn't understand that she was not the proper match for Demetrius. She was flawed and she just couldn't put Demetrius through the same agony she endured day in and day out as she watched her mother slowly fade away.

"And now, my dear, I hate to bother you, but I have a most urgent request. Would you be willing to help out this old man?"

Zoe would never classify the vital man standing before her as old. She had no idea what he was about to ask of her, but she didn't have it in her to turn him down.

"Of course. Just tell me what you need me to do."

CHAPTER TWENTY

Z OE WAS ON a special mission—a royal mission.

She sat alone in the back of a limo.

The car pulled to a stop in front of the Mirraccino Royal Hospital. The driver opened the door for her. *Here goes nothing.*

Zoe stuck one shiny, red-heeled boot on the pavement. Then the other. What had possessed her to agree to this? Okay, so it wasn't every day the king asked her for a favor. Oh boy, what a favor.

Taking a deep breath, she stood up. She automatically reached down and gave a tug on the snug-fitting green velvet skirt with a jagged hem that stopped just above her knees. The neckline was scooped with red fringe and gold jingle bells. A red belt with a large gold buckle held everything in place. And a matching red velvet shrug sweater with three-quarter-length sleeves kept away the chill in the December air. The hat was really special in a unique kind of way. It was made of the same red-and-green material as the dress, but what was worse were the two or three dozen jingle bells sewn all around it. With every move she made, her head jingled and heads turned her way. Oh, the things the spectators must be thinking.

When she told the king that she'd do him this favor, she'd imagined handing out gifts in her normal street clothes. She didn't recall the king mentioning anything about dressing up like an elf. But then there'd been a special box delivered to her apartment that afternoon with her name on it. Inside she'd found the outfit and a note with the king's crest on the front. She'd opened the note card to find a hand-scrawled message that simply said, *"Grazie."*

The limo driver removed a red sack from the trunk. When he returned to her side, she said, "I can take it."

The driver's gaze moved from her to the sack. "It's my job."

It didn't look too heavy and the car was currently parked in the fire zone. "I insist." She held out her hand. "I've got it from here."

The driver looked torn. "You're sure?"

She nodded. "I appreciate the ride."

The man in the black suit and driver's cap handed over the Santa sack full of what she suspected were toys. And though it weighed a little more than she anticipated, she could manage on her own.

The driver cleared his throat. "They're expecting you on the fifth floor. Just follow the sound of excited voices."

Zoe thanked the kind man again, slung the pack over her shoulder and set off. *Jingle. Jingle. Jingle.* Women smiled. Men stared—some even winked. Thank goodness Demetrius wasn't here to witness her experience as an elf. She'd never live it down—then again, it was highly doubtful that he'd speak to her again.

The driver's directions were perfect. She easily found the Christmas party. The large room was filled with an army of wheelchairs holding excited children who were all chattering at once. At the front of the room sat a very plump Santa in a red velvet outfit with lush white fur trim. Santa's deep ho-ho-ho boomed across the room as he held a hand over his round belly that was strapped in with a wide black belt.

"She's here! She's here!" Cheers filled the room.

They were all waiting for her? As everyone turned her way, heat rushed to her cheeks. She'd be willing to bet if she checked a mirror that her face was as red as Santa's suit.

"Annabelle, we've been waiting for you." Santa's voice

was deep but there was a familiar tone to it. When she stopped next to Jolly Saint Nick and slung her load to the floor, he leaned over and said softly, "You're certainly not Annabelle. What are you doing here?"

Now Zoe knew why that voice sounded so familiar. Behind that bushy beard, gold-rimmed glasses and makeup was Demetrius. Her heart clenched. Had the king known his son would be here? Well, of course he had. He was the king.

"Your father sent me." She thought the explanation would put a quick end to his questions and they could get to work. Being so close to Demetrius and yet so far away was extremely difficult for her.

"Why would my father send you here?"

Zoe resisted the urge to sigh in frustration. "I think the kids want their presents."

"Not until you explain why he sent you."

"The king summoned me to the palace and explained how Annabelle had come down with the flu. He explained how delivering toys to the children's ward was a royal family tradition. And since he thought that Annabelle and I are about the same size, he thought that I could fill in for her."

Demetrius sent her a puzzled look. "But I just saw Annabelle this morning at the office. She looked fine. It was my father who told me he wasn't feeling well. Come to think of it, this is the first Christmas I can recall when he hasn't dressed up like Santa."

"Well, he looked fine when I talked to him." Zoe wasn't about to tell Demetrius what else they'd discussed such as her loving his son.

Demetrius's mouth opened but nothing came out.

"What?" Concern filled her. "Demetrius, what's the matter?"

"I think my father is playing matchmaker."

She'd gotten that feeling earlier at the palace, but she

never thought the king would take it this far. Her gaze lifted and met Demetrius's. Her heart pitter-pattered faster and faster. If only…

"Don't worry. I'll take care of this. I'll make it clear to my father that you and I are through." Demetrius's tone lacked emotion. And then he turned away. "Who's ready for some presents? Ho-ho-ho."

Demetrius was a far better actor than she. It took all of her determination to keep her eyes from misting up. If it wasn't for the hopeful faces and the excited voices, she'd have never made it through the afternoon.

They never had a chance to speak privately again. She told herself that it was for the best. The less contact they had the better it'd be.

But none of those excuses eased the pain. She loved Demetrius more now than the day she'd married him. And even if she didn't have the threat of that dreaded disease hanging over her head, Demetrius didn't want her. He'd finally realized she wasn't cut out to be a princess—his princess.

He couldn't get Zoe out of his thoughts.

Demetrius paced back and forth in his office. It was the only peaceful place in the palace. Tonight was the Royal Christmas Ball and he'd given the entire staff the day off in order to prepare for the big event.

"I thought I'd find you down here."

Demetrius stopped pacing and glanced up to find his twin, Alex, standing in the doorway. "When did you get back from the States?"

"Last night. I thought I'd see you at dinner—"

"I wasn't hungry." He'd barely eaten a bite since his relationship with Zoe had disintegrated right before his eyes.

"From the looks of you, I'd say along with giving up food, you've given up shaving and combing your hair."

Demetrius sent his brother a cold, hard stare. "Leave me alone."

"Not until you hear me out."

"I don't need a lecture. I need to be alone." If Alex wasn't going to leave, Demetrius would. He started for the door, but Alex moved in his way.

Alex gave him a wary look as though trying to decide if he was going to have to tackle him to the ground to make him stay in place. "It looks like I got back just in time. Someone needs to talk some sense into you."

Demetrius raked his fingers through his hair, not caring what he looked like. That was the least of his problems. "You don't know what's going on."

"Actually, I know a lot more than you think. Papa's very worried about you. He's filled me in on what he knows. What I don't understand is how a stalker reporter broke you and Zoe up."

"Do you really want to know?"

Alex nodded and Demetrius let it all spill out. His worry that the title of princess would bring more pain to Zoe's life than any joy he could give her. His fear that something would happen to Zoe like had happened to their mother. He just couldn't be responsible for any harm coming to Zoe.

Alex reached out and squeezed his shoulder. "It isn't easy. I won't pretend that love and marriage don't require putting yourself out there. If this Zoe is the right lady for you, you have to take the risk."

"But what if something happens to her? I'll never forgive myself."

"If you're looking for guarantees, there aren't any. But is it worth it to give up the woman you love over a what-if scenario?"

His brother had a point. But that wasn't the only thing eating at him. Zoe had a secret—a really big secret.

"But how am I supposed to open up to her about my

worries when she's afraid to tell me what she's most afraid of?" It tore him up that she wouldn't trust him with the information.

"It sounds like you already know what it is."

"I do. I've known for a while. She's afraid she's going to end up with Alzheimer's like her mother."

Alex didn't say anything for a moment as the news sunk in. "That's a really big deal. I can't blame her for being scared."

"But she doesn't seem to believe that part of our vows where it said 'for better or worse, in sickness and in health.'"

Alex arched a brow. "So you're saying that no matter what, you're going to love her?"

"*Sì.*" There was no hesitation in his answer—none whatsoever.

"Then go tell her what you just told me. Nothing important in life comes easily—at least not in my experience. Trust me. I almost let the woman I love slip through my fingers. The best approach is to be up-front and honest. You can't attempt to solve the problem until you both have it all out there in the open. Let her know that you love her and that you aren't going anywhere."

Demetrius knew that his twin was right. But would Zoe hear him out?

Alex cleared his throat, regaining Demetrius's attention. "Is winning Zoe back truly what you want?"

"*Sì.*" He'd never been more certain about anything. "She's the one and only for me. And if she'll have me, I plan to have our wedding vows renewed."

CHAPTER TWENTY-ONE

Since when had Alex become a relationship expert?

Obviously Alex's wife had taught him some important lessons.

Demetrius rushed through the shower, shaved his three-day beard and threw on his tux. On his ride to the ball, he finally checked his messages. He found a text from Zoe saying she wouldn't be attending the ball. He redirected the car to her apartment.

It was his fault that she'd be missing her chance to shine like the star that she was both inside and out. She was amazing. And thanks to his brother, Demetrius realized that he'd been a fool to let her go.

Certain that she loved him, he just had to find her. It was past time they got everything out in the open, including her secret. Even if she'd been diagnosed with the Alzheimer's gene like her mother, it wouldn't change the way he felt about her. The thought of her being ill was painful but what was even more painful was the thought of wasting all of the good days they could have together—talking, laughing—just being in each other's company.

He rushed up the steps of her apartment building and stopped in front of her door. It was only then that he realized he shouldn't have showed up empty-handed. He should have brought flowers—roses—red roses. That's what women liked, wasn't it?

Oh, well, it was too late to worry about it now. Tomorrow he'd place an order with the florist to have flowers delivered to Zoe every month or every week, whatever made her happy. He clenched his hand and knocked. She just had to be there.

Almost immediately the door swung open. An older woman stood there with a very surprised look on her face. He'd seen that look on many faces when people recognized him. Her mouth opened but nothing came out. This must be the friend Zoe mentioned that was helping out with her mother.

He sent her a friendly smile, hoping to gain an ally. "Hello. Is Zoe at home?"

The woman smiled back at him and shook her head.

"Who is it? Who's at the door?" Another woman made her way across the living room to join them. The woman had gray streaking through her dark hair. She most definitely resembled Zoe. This had to be her mother. So this was what Zoe would look like when she got older. Still beautiful.

Lines creased between her brows. Zoe's mother studied his face as though she should know him, but she couldn't quite place his face. "Do I know you?"

"I don't think that I've had the pleasure. I'm Prince Demetrius."

The title didn't seem to faze Zoe's mother. "Are you a friend of my daughter?"

Demetrius's gaze moved to the other woman, looking for direction. She shrugged, leaving him on his own. He turned back to Zoe's mother. "*Sì.* She's very special to me."

"Don't you hurt my Zoe. You hear?" The woman sent him a no-nonsense look.

"I'll do my best not to." But he knew that he'd already failed that request.

Confusion clouded her eyes. "Who are you?"

"Prince Demetrius."

The other woman held up a finger, signaling for him to wait.

He nodded in understanding. The woman escorted Zoe's mother to the couch before returning to the door.

"Thanks for being so understanding. I take it you know about her condition."

"Zoe told me."

"Well, Zoe didn't tell me about you." The woman ran a hand over her hair. "Oh, my goodness. Where are my manners? I'm Liliana, a friend of the family."

"It's nice to meet you. About Zoe, do you know where she is?"

"She's at the ball. I insisted she go after how hard she worked. This is her night to shine—"

"*Grazie.* I'm sorry to rush off, but it's urgent that I speak with her."

The woman smiled. "Tell Zoe not to worry about coming home tonight. I have everything under control."

"I will."

Not about to let the princess of his heart get away, Demetrius set off after her.

She shouldn't have come.

Zoe was in no mood for a party. In fact, that afternoon she'd escorted her mother to a doctor's appointment. The doctor had urged her to get her mother situated in Residenza del Rosa as soon as possible. He assured her that it would be better for her mother in the long run. She'd feel more settled as the disease progressed.

Though Zoe wanted to argue with the doctor, she couldn't. Her mother had told her at the beginning of this journey that she never wanted to be a burden on Zoe. The day had just arrived far sooner than Zoe had expected. She wasn't ready to let go. But her mother had squeezed her hand and told her it would be all right. Next week, her mother would move in to Residenza del Rosa—her new home.

Zoe was set to cancel her plans and stay home tonight, but her mother and Liliana insisted they wanted to see her in the gown. She'd picked it out special with Demetrius in mind.

She tugged at her burgundy taffeta gown. She glanced down wondering if the strapless, sweetheart neckline embellished with delicate crystals dipped a bit too low. The problem was she just wasn't used to being all gussied up in an A-line gown that hugged all of her curves with a gentle ruching at her hips.

She hoped it didn't make her look fat. She sucked in her stomach a little more, hoping it would help. Her mother and their friend assured her that she looked wonderful, but she didn't trust either of them. They'd say that even if her face was breaking out and she was wearing an old sack.

"You showed up."

Zoe didn't even have to turn around. She recognized the voice. It was Demetrius. She hadn't seen him since they'd posed as Santa and his trusty elf.

She turned to him and was immediately struck by how handsome he looked in his black tux. His hair was perfectly styled. Her fingers tingled with the urge to reach out and stroke his freshly shaven jaw. She resisted the temptation.

She swallowed hard. "Bet you're surprised to see me here after the message I sent you."

"More like relieved."

Relieved? That was a good sign, wasn't it? She glanced around the crowded room, wondering if there were photographers lurking about just waiting to catch a picture of them together. "Do you think it's a good idea to be seen talking to me?"

"The first thing to learn about dealing with the paparazzi is not to let them dictate your life. Otherwise, I'd never leave the palace. If they want to create a story, they will with or without any help."

She supposed he was right, but that didn't put her at ease. The last thing she needed was the paparazzi digging around in her life. She already had too much going on with the pending annulment and her mother's care.

"Zoe, stop worrying. I made sure the press wasn't allowed into the ball tonight."

"You did?" Her eyes widened. "But I thought you wanted as much press coverage as possible for the project."

"Not at the expense of your happiness. I'll still make sure there's plenty of coverage, just not tonight." Demetrius moved closer and placed a finger beneath her chin, tilting it up. "Are you okay?"

"Um…*sì*." Definitely better now that he was there.

"You look a little pale. Did you eat anything today?"

She shrugged. "I had a little."

He sent her an I-don't-believe-you look.

The truth was she hadn't had more than *caffè* and toast that morning. She'd been worried about her mother's appointment and then the thought of fitting into her gown. And now with Demetrius standing before her looking like he'd just stepped off the cover of a glossy magazine, her stomach felt as though it were filled with a swarm of fluttering butterflies.

"That dress looks amazing on you." His smile succeeded in increasing the fluttering sensation in her stomach.

"You're the one who looks amazing. You were born to wear a tux."

"*Grazie*." He gave a tug on each sleeve. "It takes years of experience to properly pull off the look."

She grinned, enjoying the fact that he was in a good mood. After all of his hard work, he deserved to enjoy this success. "You shouldn't be wasting time with me."

"It's definitely not a waste of time. I can't think of any place I'd rather be."

"But you have important guests to entertain. You need their support to continue the project."

"Don't worry. There's plenty of time for all of that."

"Demetrius, I need to apologize. I want to explain—"

"Shh…we'll talk. We have all night. Liliana said she doesn't expect to see you tonight. She has everything under control."

"You saw Liliana and…and my mother?"

He nodded. "I went looking for you."

"But why?"

"Because you're my date for tonight. And now it's my turn to ask you a question. Can I have this dance?"

Heat rushed up her neck and warmed her cheeks. There was music playing? She hadn't noticed until he'd mentioned it. Demetrius held out his arm to her and suddenly she felt like Cinderella at the ball.

Oh, what would it hurt to enjoy herself for the evening in the arms of the most amazing man in the world? She accepted his arm. He escorted her onto the busy dance floor. She didn't even want to contemplate the number of women who would die to be in her place, much less be the wife of this amazing prince. She'd pinch herself to make sure this was all real, but she didn't want to remove her hands from him—afraid he might disappear again.

As the eighteen-piece orchestra played, Demetrius skillfully guided her around the dance floor. She'd swear that her feet never even touched the floor. She smiled and smiled until her cheeks hurt, and then she smiled some more.

Throughout it all, she didn't let herself think about what would happen when the clock struck twelve. The whole world slipped away, leaving just the two of them swaying gently to the music. She never wanted to let him go.

Demetrius stared deep into her eyes. "Close your eyes."

Instead of arguing and questioning him as she normally

would do, she simply closed her eyes, trusting him to guide her safely around the room.

Demetrius pulled her closer. "Now imagine that my lips are pressed to yours."

She could visualize his face and how he would lean over to her. She could imagine his lips pressed to hers. A wishful sigh crossed her lips.

"Imagine me pulling you close. Real close. Our bodies press together. My lips moving over yours. You taste sweet as *vino*. No. Sweeter." His voice was warm and soft, for her ears only. "I can't stop kissing you."

Was he really seducing her here on the dance floor? Because if so, it was working. Heat rushed up her neck, setting her whole face ablaze. Her eyes sprang open.

"Hey, no cheating. Close your eyes."

It was as though his touch and the deep tones of his voice had a spell over her. She once again did as he asked, eagerly wondering where this fantasy was to take them next. Her mind started to jump ahead quite a few steps. It was getting warm in there. Very warm indeed.

"My lips are still on yours." He pulled her closer. His lips were next to her ear. His breath brushed lightly over her neck. "My fingers work their way up your back until they are plucking the pins from your hair and letting your curls fall down over your shoulders."

The breath hitched in her throat as she waited for his next words. "And…"

He chuckled. "Anxious, aren't you?"

She smiled. "Definitely."

"My lips trail over your cheek and over to your ear where I whisper a few sweet nothings. And then I move down to that sensitive spot on your neck. You know, the spot that drives you wild."

Goose bumps trailed down her arms as she recalled the delicious sensations that he could arouse. "And then what?"

CHAPTER TWENTY-TWO

BEFORE HE COULD say another word, the music stopped. Zoe's eyes opened. *Not yet.* She resisted the urge to stomp her feet in frustration. Things were just getting good. Who knew that Demetrius could play out a seduction scene so smoothly?

"Quit pouting," he whispered in her ear as he led her from the dance floor. "We aren't finished."

"We aren't?" She knew that she shouldn't be so eager, but she just couldn't help herself.

"If you eat something, we'll continue this fantasy."

She still didn't have much of an appetite. "Does chocolate count?"

His lips pressed together as he considered her request. "How about some crackers and cheese with a side of chocolate?"

"If I must." Crackers actually didn't sound so bad, after all.

"Good. Why don't you go wait for me out on the terrace? We should have some privacy there and then I might do more than just talk."

"Promise?"

His eyes glittered with unspoken promises. "I do."

As he walked away, her feet came back down to earth. As much as it pained her to admit, she couldn't let this fantasy go on. It'd be too painful when it was over. When he returned, she steeled herself to be brutally honest with him. He deserved to know what he was getting himself into.

A couple of minutes later, he joined her in the cool evening air. Luckily, no one had decided to come outside to admire the stars. They had the whole terrace to themselves.

He handed her a plate of finger foods. "Here you go. Make sure you eat the crackers."

"But there's something I need to tell you first. Something I should have told you a long time ago."

The smile slid from his face. "If this is about you inheriting Alzheimer's, I know."

She set aside the plate. "You know?"

He nodded. "And it doesn't matter. I just wish you'd have told me sooner."

"I couldn't, because I knew you'd do this. You'd be a knight in shining armor and do the gentlemanly thing."

"Which is what?"

She pressed her hands to her hips and lifted her chin. "You'd say that none of this matters. That we can do anything as long as we're together."

He couldn't help but smile just a bit. "That is exactly what I'd say. And I'd be right."

She shook her head. "Stop being so gallant. You have more than yourself to think about. You're the prince. The future ruler of Mirraccino. You are expected to produce the next heir to the throne."

"And…"

"And I can't give you that heir. Don't you see, I have a fifty-fifty chance of inheriting the same disease? I can't— I won't pass that on to my children."

His brows drew together. "So you don't know if you have the disease?"

She shook her head. "There's DNA testing, but I haven't had it done yet."

"Why not?"

Her voice grew soft, hating to have to admit this to a man who never had to inquire about the price before purchasing whatever his heart desired. "I couldn't afford the tests.

My mother's medical expenses take everything I earn." But aside from the cost, she was afraid. "And I didn't know if I could deal with the results while I was watching what it was doing to my mother. She needed all of my focus and positivity."

"And this design job—"

"I needed it in order to pay for my mother's care. Her doctor has been warning us that the time was coming when she'd need more than I could give her while holding down a job. My mother insisted all along that she didn't want me caring for her to the end. I thought that if she could stay here at Residenza del Rosa that it would be close enough to the apartment that I could visit her every day."

Demetrius nodded as though at last the pieces of the puzzle were falling into place. "I just wish that you would have trusted me. I would have helped you through all of this."

She blinked repeatedly. "It isn't you I didn't trust. It was me. I'd been running so long, so hard that I didn't know if I could be the strong, sturdy person that my mother needs me to be."

"It looks to me like you're an amazing daughter."

"I'm doing my best. I was trying to protect you, too. I didn't want to become a burden to you. You have a country to run—people counting on you—"

He reached out, cupping his hands over her shoulders. "Don't you know by now that there's nothing and no one more important to me than you? I love you. I have since the day we met."

That was it. The dam broke. She lowered her head as a tear splashed onto her cheek. "I love you, too. But you would be better off without me. I'm all wrong to be a princess."

"I disagree." His thumb moved beneath her chin and lifted her head until he was looking into her eyes. "I can't think of anyone who would fit the position better."

"What? No. You can't be serious."

"I'm very serious."

He wasn't thinking this through. "What if I have this disease? What if I can't—won't—have kids?"

"Then my brother and his kids will inherit the crown."

This couldn't be happening. He really wanted her, flaws and all. "But I'm a commoner. I have no money, no influence, and no important ties to any foreign countries."

"You have something more important. You are the bravest person I know. You took on the world by yourself in order to care for your mother. You have a heart of gold—always putting the happiness of others ahead of your own. And you aren't afraid of hard work. Just look at this place, it's amazing."

"Really?" When he nodded, she continued. "You aren't just saying that to make me feel better? You thought about this?"

"I haven't thought of anything else. I mean every word I've said. I'm the luckiest man in the world."

Her heart swelled with the warmth of love radiating from Demetrius. "What does this mean?"

He gazed deeply into her eyes. "It means I love you with all of my heart. I can't imagine my life without you in it."

"I love you, too. I never stopped."

His hand moved, allowing the backs of his fingers to swipe away her tears. His head dipped, and then his lips claimed hers. She leaned into him. At last, she knew where she belonged. She didn't know how the next chapter of her life would end, but she now knew how it would start.

Demetrius stopped kissing her and leaned his forehead against hers. "Come inside with me so we can announce our marriage. I want everyone to know how lucky I am."

"What about the annulment papers?"

"Did I forget to tell you that I accidentally dropped

them? They landed in the paper shredder. So it looks like you're stuck with me."

Her vision blurred with tears of joy. "So we're still married?"

"That we are. You are now and always will be the princess of my heart."

EPILOGUE

A year later...

"YOU DO KNOW that you're breaking with tradition?"

Demetrius strode into the palace library, finding his wife standing on a step stool with a red shimmery ornament in her hand. He'd never imagined that he could fall more in love with her, but each day that passed, he found himself falling further and further under her spell. And he couldn't be happier.

Zoe glanced over her shoulder at him. "I just need to find a spot for this last ornament."

Demetrius's gaze reluctantly moved to the Christmas tree. White twinkle lights shimmered off the dozens of ornaments. "I don't think there's room for more."

"Sure there is." Zoe sounded so confident. "There's always room for more."

He smiled and shook his head at her determination.

Over the past year, so many things had changed. First, they had a splashy wedding to the thrill of the people of Mirraccino—and Zoe, who got to wear a white dress with a long train. After which Zoe decided to get the DNA testing done. There had been some long sleepless nights while they both waited for the results, but to everyone's relief, Zoe hadn't inherited her mother's early onset familial Alzheimer's.

And though they'd moved into the palace and Demetrius was fully immersed in matters of state, his father still refused to step down from the throne, even though his doctors had advised him that it would be best for his heart. Demetrius now knew where he'd inherited his stubborn streak. All he could do was be there to alleviate as much of the stress as he could until his father was willing to see reason.

Zoe held up the sparkly Christmas ornament, regaining his attention. She'd never been more beautiful. He'd swear she was glowing with happiness. She moved the decoration around, still trying to decide which limb to place it on. At last satisfied, she situated it near the top.

She turned to him, resting a hand atop her slightly rounded belly. Her face was radiant. "It's time we started a new tradition. After all, you helped me decorate the tree last year and you didn't do such a bad job."

"Hey! I did a really good job. You said it was the prettiest tree you'd ever seen."

She arched a brow. "I think they call that revising the past."

He approached her, finding himself unable to keep his hands to himself whenever she was in the room with him. "Maybe you should come down here so we can discuss these new traditions."

She smiled and stepped down the little ladder until she was standing on the lowest rung. Her eyes twinkled with merriment. "Why, Prince Demetrius, if I didn't know better, I'd think that you have a lot more on your mind than talking."

He wrapped his hands around her expanding waistline and lifted her to him. Her body slid down over his. His pulse raced. It didn't matter how long they were together, he couldn't imagine ever being immune to her charms.

Her arms looped around his neck as she gazed deep into his eyes. "You do know that we're expected at Residenza del Rosa soon, don't you? I want to take my mum her presents. I called and this is one of her better days."

He had to hand it to his wife. She was the strongest person he'd ever known. Though her mother's condition was deteriorating, Zoe did her best to stay positive even though her mother recognized her less and less. On the days when Zoe needed a hug, a shoulder to lean on or an ear to listen, he made sure to be there for her. She was his priority. It wasn't all sunshine and roses, but together they were getting through the challenges life threw at them.

"Don't worry. We won't be late. In fact, I think we have just enough time to squeeze in a little of this." His lips pressed to hers. He knew from plenty of experience that it wouldn't take much to sway her into delaying their outing.

"Hey, isn't that how you two got in trouble already?"

With great reluctance, Demetrius released his princess and turned to face his brother. "I don't think you have any room to talk."

"Is my husband causing problems already?" Reese entered the room wearing a blue cotton top with the words Precious Cargo Aboard emblazoned across her rounded midsection.

Demetrius smiled. "He's always causing trouble."

"Don't I know it." Reese pressed a hand to her back. "Did he tell you yet?"

"Tell us what?" Zoe spoke up.

"That he's been up to his antics." Reese frowned at her prince, but her eyes said that she was only playing with him. "It appears that we're not having a baby boy, we're having two—boys that is."

"That's wonderful." Zoe rushed over to hug her.

Demetrius gave Zoe a look. "You aren't carrying twins, too, are you?"

She started to laugh. "Not me. But I do have a surprise."

"I love surprises." The king entered the room. A smile lit up his face. He looked so much more at ease now that both of his sons were taking on a lot of the workload that the king had shouldered for so long on his own. "Well, don't keep us in suspense."

Zoe smiled at her father-in-law. Over this past year they'd grown quite close as they took daily strolls through the flower gardens. Demetrius always wondered what they found to talk about, but he didn't want to pry. Some things were best left alone.

Zoe moved to Demetrius's side. "I was planning to save this announcement for Christmas day, but now seems rather fitting."

Demetrius's chest tightened. "You're starting to worry me. Nothing is wrong, is it?"

She smiled and shook her head. "Everything is fine. Do you think Mirraccino is ready for a queen that looks like me and acts like you?"

He breathed easier. "It's a girl?"

She nodded. Demetrius picked her up and swung her around. He didn't care whether it was a little boy or girl just so long as baby and mom were both healthy. "Hey, you cheated. You weren't supposed to consult the doctor while I was off on that business trip to Milan."

Zoe glanced away. "I… I had some pains—"

"What? Why is this the first I'm hearing of it?"

She pressed a hand to his chest where his heart was pounding as adrenaline raced through his veins. Nothing could be wrong with them. He didn't know what he'd do if he lost Zoe after everything they'd gone through.

"Relax." Her voice was soft and comforting. "The doctor told me that it was normal. They were growing pains. Completely natural."

"You're sure?"

She nodded. "He even did a sonogram to assure me everything was fine." She moved to her purse that was on the couch and pulled something out. "Meet your daughter."

Demetrius stared at the photo and then at his wife. His vision blurred a bit, but he didn't care in the least. He couldn't believe that he'd been so blessed.

"This is going to be the best Christmas ever."

With that he pulled his wife into his arms and kissed her, leaving no doubt about how much he loved her. Now and forever.

* * * * *

MILLS & BOON®
Hardback – November 2015

ROMANCE

A Christmas Vow of Seduction	Maisey Yates
Brazilian's Nine Months' Notice	Susan Stephens
The Sheikh's Christmas Conquest	Sharon Kendrick
Shackled to the Sheikh	Trish Morey
Unwrapping the Castelli Secret	Caitlin Crews
A Marriage Fit for a Sinner	Maya Blake
Larenzo's Christmas Baby	Kate Hewitt
Bought for Her Innocence	Tara Pamm
His Lost-and-Found Bride	Scarlet Wilson
Housekeeper Under the Mistletoe	Cara Colter
Gift-Wrapped in Her Wedding Dress	Kandy Shepherd
The Prince's Christmas Vow	Jennifer Faye
A Touch of Christmas Magic	Scarlet Wilson
Her Christmas Baby Bump	Robin Gianna
Winter Wedding in Vegas	Janice Lynn
One Night Before Christmas	Susan Carlisle
A December to Remember	Sue MacKay
A Father This Christmas?	Louisa Heaton
A Christmas Baby Surprise	Catherine Mann
Courting the Cowboy Boss	Janice Maynard

MILLS & BOON®
Large Print – November 2015

ROMANCE

he Ruthless Greek's Return	Sharon Kendrick
ound by the Billionaire's Baby	Cathy Williams
larried for Amari's Heir	Maisey Yates
Taste of Sin	Maggie Cox
icilian's Shock Proposal	Carol Marinelli
ows Made in Secret	Louise Fuller
he Sheikh's Wedding Contract	Andie Brock
Bride for the Italian Boss	Susan Meier
he Millionaire's True Worth	Rebecca Winters
he Earl's Convenient Wife	Marion Lennox
ettori's Damsel in Distress	Liz Fielding

HISTORICAL

Rose for Major Flint	Louise Allen
he Duke's Daring Debutante	Ann Lethbridge
ord Laughraine's Summer Promise	Elizabeth Beacon
Varrior of Ice	Michelle Willingham
Wager for the Widow	Elisabeth Hobbes

MEDICAL

lways the Midwife	Alison Roberts
lidwife's Baby Bump	Susanne Hampton
Kiss to Melt Her Heart	Emily Forbes
empted by Her Italian Surgeon	Louisa George
aring to Date Her Ex	Annie Claydon
he One Man to Heal Her	Meredith Webber

EN STD LP

MILLS & BOON®
Hardback – December 2015

ROMANCE

The Price of His Redemption	Carol Marinelli
Back in the Brazilian's Bed	Susan Stephens
The Innocent's Sinful Craving	Sara Craven
Brunetti's Secret Son	Maya Blake
Talos Claims His Virgin	Michelle Smart
Destined for the Desert King	Kate Walker
Ravensdale's Defiant Captive	Melanie Milburne
Caught in His Gilded World	Lucy Ellis
The Best Man & The Wedding Planner	Teresa Carpenter
Proposal at the Winter Ball	Jessica Gilmore
Bodyguard...to Bridegroom?	Nikki Logan
Christmas Kisses with Her Boss	Nina Milne
Playboy Doc's Mistletoe Kiss	Tina Beckett
Her Doctor's Christmas Proposal	Louisa George
From Christmas to Forever?	Marion Lennox
A Mummy to Make Christmas	Susanne Hampton
Miracle Under the Mistletoe	Jennifer Taylor
His Christmas Bride-to-Be	Abigail Gordon
Lone Star Holiday Proposal	Yvonne Lindsay
A Baby for the Boss	Maureen Child

MILLS & BOON®
Large Print – December 2015

ROMANCE

The Greek Demands His Heir	Lynne Graham
The Sinner's Marriage Redemption	Annie West
His Sicilian Cinderella	Carol Marinelli
Captivated by the Greek	Julia James
The Perfect Cazorla Wife	Michelle Smart
Claimed for His Duty	Tara Pammi
The Marakaios Baby	Kate Hewitt
Return of the Italian Tycoon	Jennifer Faye
His Unforgettable Fiancée	Teresa Carpenter
Hired by the Brooding Billionaire	Kandy Shepherd
A Will, a Wish...a Proposal	Jessica Gilmore

HISTORICAL

Griffin Stone: Duke of Decadence	Carole Mortimer
Rake Most Likely to Thrill	Bronwyn Scott
Under a Desert Moon	Laura Martin
The Bootlegger's Daughter	Lauri Robinson
The Captain's Frozen Dream	Georgie Lee

MEDICAL

Midwife...to Mum!	Sue MacKay
His Best Friend's Baby	Susan Carlisle
Italian Surgeon to the Stars	Melanie Milburne
Her Greek Doctor's Proposal	Robin Gianna
New York Doc to Blushing Bride	Janice Lynn
Still Married to Her Ex!	Lucy Clark

MILLS & BOON®

Why shop at millsandboon.co.uk?

Each year, thousands of romance readers find their perfect read at millsandboon.co.uk. That's because we're passionate about bringing you the very best romantic fiction. Here are some of the advantages of shopping at www.millsandboon.co.uk:

* **Get new books first**—you'll be able to buy your favourite books one month before they hit the shops

* **Get exclusive discounts**—you'll also be able to buy our specially created monthly collections, with up to 50% off the RRP

* **Find your favourite authors**—latest news, interviews and new releases for all your favourite authors and series on our website, plus ideas for what to try next

* **Join in**—once you've bought your favourite books, don't forget to register with us to rate, review and join in the discussions

Visit **www.millsandboon.co.uk**
for all this and more today!